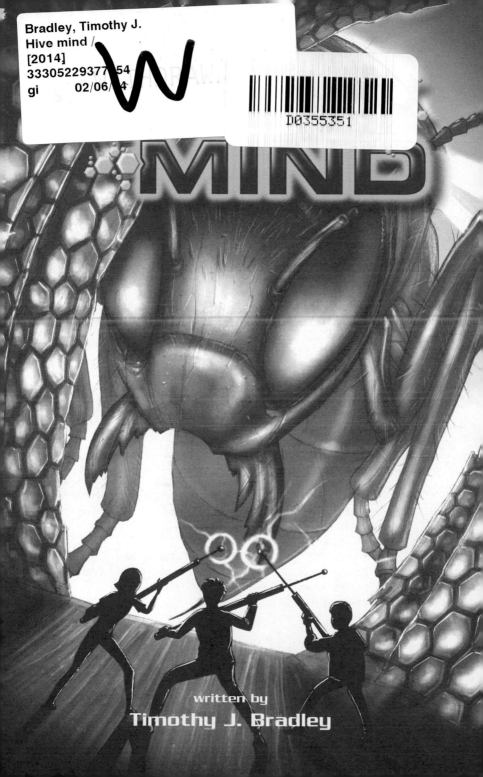

MIND

written by

Timothy J. Bradley

This is a work of fiction. Names, characters, places, and incidents are either products of the author's imagination or, if real, are used fictitiously.

First paperback edition

The library of Congress has catalogued the paperback edition as follows:
Bradley, Timothy J.
Hive mind / by Timothy J. Bradley—First paperback edition.
pages cm
Summary: Thirteen-year-old Sidney Jamison is bored with school and getting in trouble for taking apart household appliances, but everything changes when he transfers to Sci Hi, where students play Zero-G dodgeball and work together to solve such real-world problems as colony collapse disorder.
ISBN 978-1-4807-2188-3 (paperback)
ISBN 978-1-4807-2612-3 (hardcover)
ISBN 978-1-4333-8787-6 (eBook)
[1. High schools—Fiction. 2. Schools—Fiction. 3. Honeybee—Fiction. 4. Bees—Fiction. 5. Science fiction.] I. Title.
PZ7.B7258Hiv 2013
[Fic]—dc23
2013019934

Argosy Press
5301 Oceanus Drive
Huntington Beach, California 92649
A division of Teacher Created Materials

The intoxicating scent of prey led the hornet into the pine trees. It flew fiercely through the warm spring morning, driven forward by a gust of wind.

Drawing closer, the hornet landed on a nearby branch and studied its target. The beehive was buzzing with activity as workers came and went, carrying pollen from distant flowers. The bees had no idea they were being watched. Or that they were about to be slaughtered.

The hornet flew closer to the hive, its wings making a deep, raspy hum. It touched down at the entrance of the hive, scraping its chemical scent onto the edge of the nest. In a flash, the odor hit them, and the bees pivoted toward the hornet, antennae twitching in alarm. The hive was already coated with the smell of death. It would not survive another attack.

CHAPTER 1

A tiny screw, a metal bracket, and a mysterious pulsing wire taunted Sidney from his desk, which was littered with nanocircuits, a sonic welder, and other tools.

Leftover parts are never a good thing, thirteen-year-old Sidney Jamison thought. He pushed his dark, curly hair out of his eyes and touched the smooth, glossy case of his mom's new voxpod. It should have blinked to life with lights and sound, but nothing happened. He looked accusingly at the three "extra" parts sitting nearby.

Curious about how the thing worked, he had taken it apart last night after his mom dozed off. He had tried to put it back together before she needed to send another message on it. *That's not going to happen now*, he thought. *I'm doomed.*

Sidney glanced around his messy room. Clothes, manuals, and half-assembled projects were strewn everywhere. There were plenty of places to hide the voxpod until he could figure out the best way to break the news to his mom without getting killed—or worse, grounded with no intermaze access.

A brisk knock at the door startled him. The door opened, and his mom stuck her head in. "Sidney, why are you still in your pajamas? We have to get moving, or—" She saw the half-assembled device on his desk. "Is that my *new voxpod*?!?!"

The doorbell rang and Sidney jumped up, relieved for the escape. "I'll get it!" He squeezed past his mom and ran for the front door.

"I don't understand why you can't just take apart your own things…." his mom sputtered as she collected the voxpod pieces and strode into the bathroom to get ready for work. As he ran for the door, Sid could hear Housemate giving his mom the daily data download as the house's digital brain set the shower temperature to her liking.

Sidney knew the punishment about to be dropped square on his head was only being postponed for lack of time. He had a long history of dismantling household appliances, from his nanobot to the autopilot on the hoverboard that was his ninth birthday present. His track record of successfully reassembling these objects was less impressive. But when he saw his mom's brand-new voxpod, the idea of cracking open the deep red shell to see how it worked was irresistible. Sidney thought if he rooted it, he could get it to project 3-D holograms. He had visions of a hologram version of himself studiously doing homework while the real Sid was outside exploring much more interesting stuff. But first things first: He had wanted to see *how* it could do that.

The outer case of the voxpod had popped open easily, and big letters had formed in the air over the device. **DO NOT ATTEMPT TO SERVICE THIS UNIT. RETURN TO THE MANUFACTURER FOR REPAIR OR THE UNIT'S WARRANTY WILL BE VOID**. Sid hadn't let the warning stop him. *They'll never know I even opened it up*, he had thought. He had been sure he could reassemble the little device. How hard could it be? Well, apparently harder than he had realized.

Now, Sidney activated the door monitor to see who had rung the bell. Nobody was visible, so he pressed the intercom button. "Hello? Who's there?"

A small metal claw rose into view and waved. "Origins: Postal Service. Delivery for Sidney Jamison."

"For me?" Sid pulled open the door to see a delivery robot that came up to his chest. Several cameras and sensors were mounted on its small, flat head. The head was balanced on a fat wheel lined with deep treads.

One of the robot's three large eyes scanned Sidney's face. "Greetings, Sidney Jamison. Delivery for you." The rapid fabricator mounted behind the robot's head started rattling. Sid watched, fascinated. His house had its own fabricator, but it was built into the framework, so he couldn't see how it worked. Ribbon cables and tubes connected a block of tiny nozzles to the robot. They moved quickly—sometimes together, sometimes separately—forming something on a tray behind the robot's head.

DING! When the fabricator finished its work, the tray rotated over the robot's head. A claw picked up the object and handed it to Sid. "Delivery complete, sir. Good-bye." And with that, the robot rolled back to the street, speeding off to its next delivery.

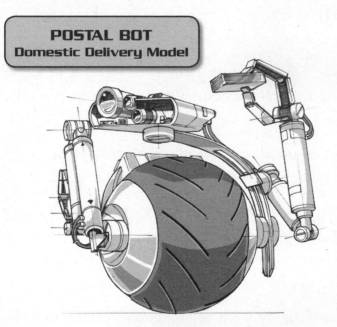

POSTAL BOT
Domestic Delivery Model

Sid looked at the translucent package in his hands. It was a flat box, about the size of a pack of playing cards, and it seemed to be made of thousands of layers of thinly sliced plastic. He turned the object over in his hands. The back flap was sealed with a foil sticker embossed with an icon of an atom. Above the seal, the words **DO NOT OPEN!** were printed.

Sid slid back into the house, still studying his delivery. He held the thing up to the light but couldn't make out any kind of detail.

"Sidney, GET DRESSED!" His mom's voice interrupted his thoughts. He must have lost track of time because his mother was staring at him with her hands on her hips. "We are leaving in *five minutes!*"

He looked down and saw his sleep shirt was now frantically blinking an alert, reminding him he was late. Sidney ran to his room, grabbed a pullover and jeans, and gave the mysterious object to the room's mechorganizer hanging from a mount in the center of the ceiling. It scanned the object and tossed it haphazardly onto the nightstand by the bed, adding to the chaos of the room. Sidney rolled his eyes and wondered if they would ever make a mechorganizer that actually organized things. Then, he dressed quickly, pulled on his racer shoes, grabbed his school voxpod, and ran downstairs.

His mom was already at the front door, giving instructions for dinner to Housemate's swiveling camera eye. "And let's have a nice salad with that, please."

The living room display wall showed the dinner menu as House replied in a pleasant voice, "Of course, Ms. Jamison. Is there anything else for today?"

"I need the national stat report loaded in my datacube. And have the plans for a new voxpod downloaded from the store and replicated for me at my office, please. Same model as the previous. Transfer all contact and user data. Deduct the cost of the new voxpod from Sidney's allowance account."

"Yes, Ms. Jamison. Have a pleasant day."

The hovercar's autodrive worked with Navcom to shuffle cars around the freeway. Their car was headed for the school, slotted into a queue along tree-lined streets. Sid's mom was still simmering about the voxpod during the drive to school. "You know, Sidney, gadgets like voxpods and macrowaves cost money. Just because we can download the infoplans and have them replicated at home doesn't make them cheap."

"Aw, mom. I just wanted to…"

"…see how it worked. I know, I know. We've had this conversation before." She sighed and switched gears. "By the way, who was at the door this morning?"

"Just a digipack," Sid said. "I'm not sure what it is. I didn't have a chance to open it yet. Probably some kind of datatrash I'll dump in the recycler."

"Interesting," his mom said. Sid didn't see her grin as she set the windshield to its mirror setting and checked her makeup. "So, what's going on at school today, kiddo?" she asked, pulling back her sandy blond hair. Her dark eyes regarded Sid with good humor. "Learning anything interesting?"

Sid rolled his eyes. "At Bleaker High? I wish. It's like sinking my brain in quicksand. Every class is just repeating stuff we learned years ago, and no one else seems to care. It's like they shut down their minds while they're at school. I'm going crazy. I mean, am I the only person in that place who can think?"

"Well, try not to let your brain get totally sucked into the quicksand. Things will change," his mom replied.

For the rest of the drive, Sid gazed out the window as gray houses and green lawns passed in a blur below him. They floated alongside the Delaware River for a few minutes, and Sid watched the nanobots rebuilding the Commodore Barry Bridge. Several months earlier, city planners had dropped twelve tons of steel and concrete at one end of the bridge and set several billion nanobots loose with instructions for remaking the structure. The nanobots had been working steadily since. They "ate" the original bridge, breaking it down as they went and leaving behind a new, stronger version. Sid could see clumps of nanobots whirling halfway along the bridge. Five minutes later, the car's airflow deflectors retracted, its wheels lowered, and the car settled onto the ground at the drop-off point.

"Bye, Mom," Sid said as he got out of the car, grabbing his bag off the seat. It contained his school voxpod and his lunch, a tuna-salad sandwich. He had eaten tuna salad every day of school since first grade, and he wasn't tired of it yet. Tuna salad was awesome.

HOVERCAR

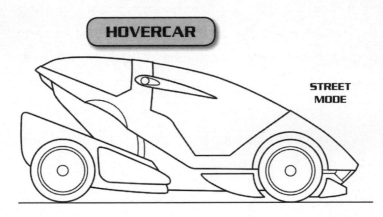

STREET
MODE

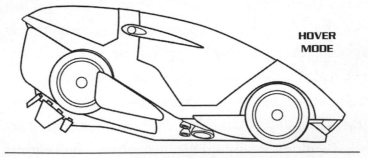

HOVER
MODE

The bell for homeroom rang as Sidney followed the other students up the drab stone steps to the tarnished metal doors of Bleaker High School. Sid heard the school's attendance computer beep as it scanned the faces of the kids filing in past its position in the ceiling just beyond the doorway. The school was as gray and weathered as the teachers, who all looked as if they struggled to stay awake as they taught the same outdated, boring material to new students each year. By the time Sidney graduated, he expected the students would take on the same grayish pallor as the teachers.

The package waiting for him at home continued to nag at Sid's brain. **DO NOT OPEN!** it had said. *Weird,* he thought and felt the beginnings of the mental itch that came on whenever he was faced with a puzzle. He couldn't get the strange instructions out of his mind, and he could barely keep himself from skipping class and sprinting home to find out what it was.

By the time science class rolled around, Sidney wasn't paying attention when Ms. Dirge called on him. "Are you listening to me, Sidney?"

"Sorry, Ms. Dirge. I didn't hear the question," Sid replied, still distracted. Ms. Dirge was an epically boring teacher. The only interesting thing he knew about her was that her mood was always reflected by the color of her face. If she was pink, she had moved past annoyed and on to frustrated. If she turned red, she was not to be messed with. One student claimed he had even seen her turn maroon once, but Sidney wasn't sure if he believed it.

"Please pay attention. I asked you to name the different stages of butterfly metamorphosis," she said sharply. Her face was beginning to flush. Her iron-gray hair twitched. "This will be on the test Friday, so you'd better know it."

Sidney groaned, frustration boiling over.

"*Know it?!* We've been studying it since *first grade*. Egg, caterpillar, chrysalis, adult! How about a bee? Egg, larva, pupa, adult! Or how about the water cycle? Evaporation, condensation, precipitation, accumulation! It's the same stuff we've been covering *every year*!"

Ms. Dirge looked at him like he was crazy, and some of the other students watched him carefully as if he had suddenly turned into a wild animal. But Sid noticed one or two kids who nodded to each other in agreement. Someone muttered, "Yeah, that's right," under his breath. *Signs of intelligent life*, Sid thought.

Encouraged, he continued. "We're not stupid. We learned all that stuff a long time ago. Why can't we learn something totally lethal for a change? Like what does zero gravity feel like? How come the sky is blue and not red? Or how come the bubbles form at the bottom of a pan when you boil water and not at the top? Why isn't there any water on Mars? What makes a spring springy? Why do different kinds of spiders spin different-shape webs? Why were some dinosaurs huge when we don't have anything *nearly* that big living now?"

His head was spinning with questions and ideas. Ms. Dirge's face was getting redder and darker, but Sid couldn't stop himself. Continuing his rant, he stood up at his desk.

"How come humans can't breathe underwater and fish can't breathe out of the water? We both need oxygen, right? Where is the moon from? What would it be like to live on Jupiter? How come glow-in-the-dark paint glows in the dark? How do bees know how to build a hive? What happens when a star explodes? Why can't we travel faster than light? What happens to water when it turns into ice? Is outer space really just empty? How can a black hole stop light from getting out?

"We keep learning the same old things the same old way! Don't you *want* us to learn so we can think for ourselves? Don't you *want* to show us how to figure things out for ourselves? *Or do you want us to be zombified sheep for the rest of our lives?*"

Sid finally slowed down enough to notice the other students were staring at him, open-mouthed. He usually never said two words in class. In fact, he thought many of his classmates had no idea who he was, even though they had been in the same classes together since kindergarten. He didn't have a lot in common with the other kids, and this probably wasn't going to help. But Sidney didn't care. School had been boring for the last nine years, and he didn't think he could take another day of it.

Then, he saw Ms. Dirge. She wasn't pink. She wasn't red. She was maroon.

The view from Principal Pritchard's office showed the sun shining down on the schoolyard. A soft breeze stirred the leaves that were turning color and just starting to drop to the ground. Inside, the principal's battered wooden desk was covered with stacks of papers and stuffed manila folders. An old computer with an actual monitor instead of a hologram display hummed to itself on a corner of the desk. There were piles of paper on the other chairs in the room and on the floor. Sidney had never seen that much paper in one place outside of a history book. He was alone, but he could hear the principal talking with Ms. Dirge outside. Their distorted shapes were visible through the frosted glass of the office door. Their voices were muffled, but their frustrated tone was clear.

"Even after skipping a year, he's just not being challenged by the material."

"I can't make the class just about Sidney Jamison."

Restless, Sidney kicked the edge of his chair and toyed with the idea of cracking open the sonic pencil sharpener on the principal's desk to see how it worked, but he stopped short when he saw his mother's car touch down in the

school parking lot. His glum mood dropped a few notches lower. *How can things get any worse?* he thought.

CHAPTER 2

Sidney knew he had screwed up royally as soon as he got in the car. His mom was quiet—too quiet.

Ellen Jamison said, "Home," her tone clipped, and the car began to move behind a line of vehicles all leaving Bleaker High on the same air track. She didn't utter a word for the first five minutes of the drive.

"All right, Mom, just say it," Sid sighed.

"Sidney, you have to control yourself in class. There's no excuse for an outburst like that," his mom lectured.

"Mom, you don't understand! We've been learning the exact same stuff *every year*," Sidney complained. "My brain's going to implode if I have to hear the words *butterfly metamorphosis* one more time. Ms. Dirge is boring to infinity."

"Well, maybe someday *you'll* be the teacher, and you'll get to call the shots. Until then, you're expected to do what the teacher tells you to do—brain implosion or not. Just give her what she wants, and you won't have any trouble. That's reasonable, isn't it?"

Sidney looked at her narrowly. "It *sounds* reasonable, but it doesn't *feel* reasonable." He sighed. She looked tired. "I hope you didn't get into trouble or anything at work."

"Well, pal, it wasn't great to get called out in the middle of a meeting," she said as she raised her eyebrows.

"Sorry. Thanks for picking me up."

"Just promise me you'll keep a handle on your temper from now on, okay?"

"Okay," Sid replied ruefully. He felt bad about ruining his mom's meeting, but he wasn't sorry for what he had said. It was all true. As they made their way home, Sidney admired the nanobot bridge. The beams glistened in the sunshine. *Maybe life would be simpler if I just act like a mindless bot and do whatever everyone else does,* he thought. The car lowered its wheels to the ground as it left the highway and started threading its way through the neighborhoods that led to the Jamisons' house. Sid brooded, staring out the window, wishing he never had to see Ms. Dirge again.

Fifteen minutes later, the car pulled into the Jamisons' driveway. As they stepped through the front door, Sid could smell the dinner Housemate was already cooking for them. The image wall in the living room displayed a slide show of family photos. Even though Sid had seen it thousands of times, it still was fun to watch his face morph from infant to toddler to tweener. The faces of family members that were no longer around were always comforting: his grandfather's smile and scratchy wool sweater; his grandmother, with her silver hair, holding a plate of cookies; and his mom and dad when they were younger. Sidney's dad had died when Sid was only two years old, so he didn't really remember him, but the photos always made Sidney feel like he was coming home to a full house.

"Good evening, Jamisons," Housemate called. "Welcome home."

"Sidney, get started on your homework, please," Ms. Jamison said.

Sidney thought about protesting but decided he was already in enough trouble. Instead, he went to his room as directed. "House, could you download my homework assignments for tonight?"

"Of course, Sidney. It is very responsible of you to get started on your homework so promptly."

Sid rolled his eyes. "Save the positive reinforcement."

"Yes, Sidney," the house answered contritely.

As he cleared his desk of tools and gadgets, he caught sight of the digipack that had come in the mail. He studied it again.

DO NOT OPEN! was printed on the face of it, yet it was sealed with nothing more than holotape.

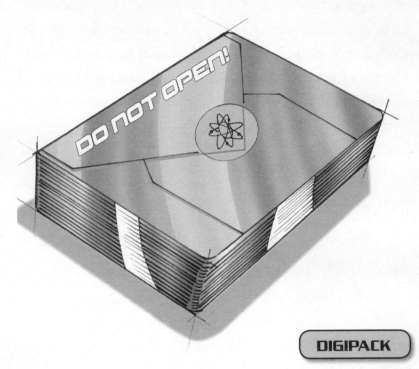

DIGIPACK

It might as well say, "Open me right now!" Sidney thought. Homework would have to wait a few minutes. His curiosity was at an epic level. He broke the seal on the back flap. Suddenly, the digipack lit up, getting brighter and brighter.

"Yikes!" Sid yelped, dropping the box on the floor. *What the heck is this thing?* he wondered.

A pinpoint of light formed above the floor, projected from the now glowing digipack. Sid stared at it, mesmerized as the tiny light grew brighter until it was almost too bright to look at. It exploded in a soundless blast that filled the room with light. Clouds of dust rushed past Sidney, swirling and expanding. Particles ignited, forming enormous stars. The entire universe seemed to spin past him. There were planets, moons, and asteroids. Galaxies swirled and dissolved. In the haze, Sidney could see one planet spinning slowly. It was Earth. Continents rushed past, giving way to cities, then neighborhoods and streets. The Jamisons' house appeared. Then the inside of the house…until Sid was staring wide-eyed at himself.

"Whoa," he breathed.

The cosmic light show suddenly disappeared. The little box on the floor was changing again, unfolding and refolding itself like some kind of glass origami. A group of sleek buildings took shape. A light shot out from the central building and spelled a greeting. "Welcome to Sci Hi," it said.

The bedroom door swung open. "What's happening in here, Sidney?" his mother asked.

"I don't know, Mom…but it's totally lethal, whatever it is!"

A powerful voice declared, "Congratulations, Sidney Lee Jamison! Only those who are curious and brave enough to open the voxvitation are offered a place at Sci Hi, the Universal High School for the Sciences."

Brave enough? Sidney wondered.

The voice continued, "We have observed your talents for many years. Your inquisitive mind and passion for discovery will serve you well at Sci Hi. If you choose to accept this invitation, you will be tackling the largest scientific problems the world has ever seen. If you decline, this message will be destroyed, and you will return to Bleaker High School, site 04937, tomorrow as scheduled.

"Please convey your decision immediately. We look forward to having you join the most creative and advanced minds on the planet."

Suddenly, the light went out.

Sidney's head was spinning. He had heard rumors about Sci Hi, but he never thought it was a real place. Nobody did. And if it did exist, he never would have thought he had a shot at actually going there. He didn't think his grades would be anywhere near high enough. Then, there was the cost. Rumor had it that Sci Hi was located on a man-made island off the coast of California. It would take a huge amount of money just to fly there, let alone live there for the school term.

He glanced up at his mom, who was standing in the doorway, grinning. "What do you think?" she asked.

"But I didn't…I'm not…How do they even know who I am?" Sid stammered.

"I'm not blind, pal. I've seen how frustrated you've been with school, so I spoke with Ms. Dirge about what we could do. She suggested Sci Hi. Ms. Dirge recommended they review your files, and she wrote a very nice letter of recommendation on your behalf."

"What?! Ms. Dirge did that for *me*?"

"We have to let them know if you're interested. What should I tell them?"

Sid was still trying to wrap his mind around what was happening. "But Mom, it's gotta be crazy expensive! How can we afford it?"

"Don't worry about that. It's well worth it if you're really interested in going there and doing your best," his mother replied.

Sidney tried to remember the whispers he had heard about Sci Hi. Different people had said different things about the school, but the basic story was the same. The school had started as an international laboratory where scientists could meet, discuss their work with one another, and conduct groundbreaking research. Sci Hi never seemed to be in the news much, but some of the rumors sounded pretty wild. Some people said the scientists there could control gravity—and even time. After years of experiments, the group had begun holding college classes for the most promising students they could find. Over time, they had started a high school to locate and educate the next generation of scientists, engineers, and technologists. The faculty was said to be made up of the world's top scientists. And the students were rumored to be the best of the best.

Even if the stories aren't really true, Sid thought, *it sure sounds cool.*

Thinking back, Sidney remembered one of the kids in his class had left suddenly without saying anything. The official story had been that he had moved to Kentucky, but Sid had also heard whispers that he had really gone to Sci Hi. At the time, the idea had seemed crazy, but now Sidney wasn't so sure.

"What do you say?" Sid's mom had out her freshly replicated voxpod, ready to call the school.

Still thunderstruck by the adventure that lay open to him, Sid just looked at her and nodded.

His mom initiated the call. "Hello? This is Ellen Jamison. I'm calling in reference to my son Sidney, who just received an invitation to attend Sci Hi...." She gave him a thumbs-up as she left the room, closing the door on the way out.

Sidney grabbed his voxpod from his desk and lay down on the carpet of his room. He said, "Search subject: Sci Hi," and set the voxpod to project the results onto the ceiling. With the voxpod resting on his stomach, Sid gazed up at the intermaze results and tried to find out what was in store for him. As he read the speculation and theories that surrounded the school, he became more and more excited. It was as if his mind had been spinning its wheels, looking for the right track, and now it had finally found its groove. He couldn't predict exactly what would happen, but he knew somehow his life was going to change at the legendary Sci Hi.

CHAPTER 3

"What time is it?" Sidney asked.

"Thirty-five seconds since the last time you asked," Housemate replied serenely.

"Very funny, House," Sid muttered. He had persuaded his mom to purchase an upgrade to Housemate's operating system that included a new sarcasm module, but he was annoyed to find he was usually the target of Housemate's remarks.

Sidney was staring out the large picture window in the living room waiting for his ride to Sci Hi. Kids from neighboring houses were playing hover hockey in the street outside. He had played a few times, usually getting stuck as goalie. He remembered being hit by the hover puck and rubbed his arm, recalling how much it stung. He wondered how long his trip would be. He expected he would have to go from his house in Philadelphia to the airport, fly to California, and then probably make some stealthy connection from that airport out to the island where the school was located. He was a bit nervous about flying, but his excitement about getting to the school overrode his apprehension about the flight.

"They'll be here, don't worry," his mom said.

Just then, a shadow fell over the house, and the leaves on the front lawn were blasted away by the arrival of the Sci Hi retrieval unit. A stealth aircraft touched down lightly on the front lawn. Silent engines on the wings and tail swiveled as they shut down, turbofans spinning.

The kids playing out in the street just stood and stared.

"Your transport has arrived," Housemate said.

"Whoa...." Sid breathed. He had been expecting a taxi or maybe a limo—not this futuristic thing. "Mom? I think my ride's here."

"Wow!" his mother said as she joined him in the living room. "Talk about traveling in style. C'mon, let's go see."

Sid grabbed his duffel bag and headed for the front door.

The door to the aircraft opened, and a short set of stairs lowered to the ground. A large robot appeared in the doorway and climbed down to the ground.

"Hello. My designation is Talos, one of the AIs assigned to Sci Hi. You must be Ellen and Sidney Jamison. A pleasure."

"Hello, um…Talos," Sid's mother said.

"What's an AI?" Sid asked.

"I am an artificial form of intelligence, a nonliving, thinking machine created to assist the scientists and researchers at Sci Hi. My duties include coordinating digital inquiries and research as well as monitoring experiments. I also enjoy chess, botany, and various forms of culinary preparation."

"You mean you like to cook? I should have you talk to our Housemate. Our dinners are getting a bit repetitious. Are you a robot?" Ms. Jamison asked.

"I am more sophisticated and complex than a robot. I am a conscious entity, just as you are. My design allows me to think beyond the parameters of my programming in order to make decisions and judgments the way the human brain does. I am a machine collective, made up of approximately thirty-five million nanobots, which allows me to alter my configuration to accomplish specialized tasks. I am the seventh of twelve AIs built at Goddard Island." Sidney raised an eyebrow at his mom, but she didn't seem to recognize the name either. "As soon as you are aboard, we will start out for the Sci Hi campus," Talos finished.

Sid gave his mom a hug. "It feels kind of strange to be going off on my own for six months."

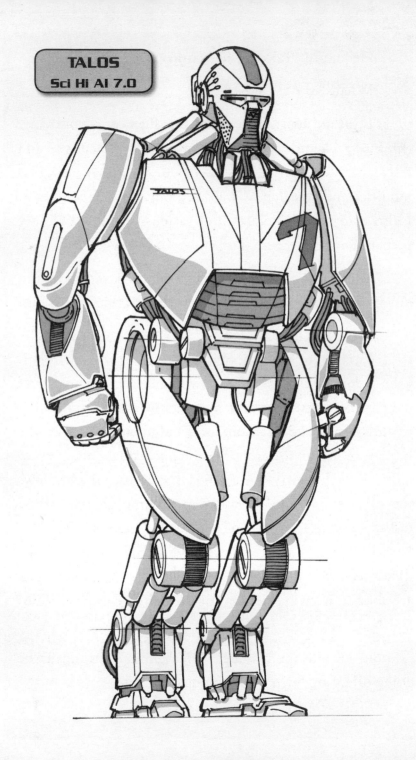

She hugged him back, holding him tightly. "You're going to have an amazing time. Just promise me you'll work hard, take apart lots of stuff, and have fun, kiddo. Call when you can." She smiled, blinking back some tears. "I'm really going to miss you."

"I'll miss you, too," Sid replied, swallowing down a hard lump in his throat. It was true. He really would miss her.

Sidney followed Talos to the gleaming jet and clambered up the steps. He turned back at the top of the stairs and took one last look at his house where his mom stood on the front lawn, waving good-bye. He tried to take a mental picture of the scene, with the old gray wooden house and their little orange car sitting in the gleaming ceramic driveway. His mom's head was tilted slightly, and her hair was blowing in the wind kicked up by the jet's engines. He tried to see Bleaker High in the distance, but it was too far away.

Things are going to be different from now on. They have to be, Sid thought, giving his mom one last wave as the steps retracted and the door to the jet closed with a thump. Taking a deep breath, he stepped into the aircraft's small, sleek passenger cabin. Soothing circles of colored light drifted along the smooth walls and ceiling. There were eight padded passenger seats, one of which was occupied by a boy who gave Sidney a nod as he entered. The boy looked about Sid's size. He had dark brown eyes, thick black hair, and skin the color of coffee. He was dressed in a wrinkled plaid shirt with his sleeves rolled up to the elbows, utility shorts, and thick-soled walking boots. Sid stashed his duffel bag under the seat and sat down next to the boy. "Hi, I'm Sid," he said, offering his hand.

"Hari," the boy said, giving him a firm handshake and a wide, friendly smile. "Nice to meet you."

"Please strap in, Sidney," Talos said from the vehicle's control cabin. "We'll be taking off in thirty seconds."

Sid buckled the safety belts across his chest and sat back in the gel-cushioned seat. The vehicle immediately lifted off, shooting straight up into the air.

"Holy smokes!" Sid yelped, gripping the armrests.

The intercom crackled to life. *"This is Talos. The Mach drive engines will be ignited shortly. We will reach our cruising speed of Mach five in ten minutes and land at Goddard Island in approximately ninety minutes."*

"Ninety minutes!" Sid exclaimed to Hari. "How can we fly from the East Coast to the West Coast that fast?"

"It only took me four hours to fly here from my home in India," Hari explained.

Sid could already feel the aircraft gathering speed. At first, the engines were roaring and the flight was choppy, but soon the engine noise quieted to a hiss and the ride became smoother. The sky outside darkened from a deep-blue color to purple as they raced through the atmosphere.

Sid turned back to Hari. "So, your family lives in India?"

Hari nodded. "My father writes software for a computer company, and my mother is a surgeon. I have an older brother named Pradeep. We live in Delhi." When Sid nodded his head, Hari continued, "My father spent some time in America, so I've been to New York and California before. They were excited that I was accepted into Sci Hi. Well, after they got over that I applied without telling them."

Sid looked at Hari with respect. "Are you kidding me? You just decided to apply…and did it? Whoa."

"My parents never would have considered sending me to Sci Hi on their own. I don't think they believed it even existed. And anyway, in my house, Pradeep is the one who gets to make all the choices, and he always chooses the safest way to get rich. He's the oldest, and my parents have very high hopes for him. They haven't given much thought to what I want to do. Up until now, I've just gone along with it. But we're in high school now. I decided this year I would do my own stuff, not just take Pradeep's leftovers. I knew if Sci Hi existed that I wanted to go there, so I searched through the intermaze for any information I could.

Somehow, they must have been alerted that I was looking for them. They sent me an application, and I filled it out and sent it in without telling anyone. Pradeep never would have done that. Once the acceptance letter came, what could they say?" Hari paused. His expression darkened. "They don't think I'll be able to cut it here. When I left, they told me to let them know when I'm ready to come home. But now that I'm going to Sci Hi, I'm not going anywhere else!"

"Oh, man! That's the complete opposite of what happened to me," Sid said. "My mom sent in the application without telling me. I never would have thought I'd be accepted. I'm no brainiac." The flight passed quickly as the boys compared stories about life in their home countries. Delhi sounded like an amazing place to grow up. Sidney tried to imagine cows walking around downtown Philly. That would be something to see.

Talos's voice once again sounded from the intercom. *If you look over the left wing, you will see the man-made island named for Robert H. Goddard, the scientist who built the first liquid-fueled rocket. We will be landing in approximately thirty seconds.*

Sid watched the island rapidly grow larger as they approached, still moving at high speed. Beaches softened the coastline, with green waves crashing on the sand. Clusters of sleek skyscrapers lined the interior of the island. In the center were the buildings that made up Sci Hi, surrounded

GODDARD ISLAND

by a ring of concrete slabs sunk into the ground. "That's the school, isn't it?" Sidney wondered. "Wow, it really does look like that voxvitation!"

"Pretty amazing, right?" Hari replied. "And that circle of concrete is where the particle accelerator is located. It's buried underground to prevent the radiation produced by the particle collisions from reaching people."

Sid could only shake his head in stunned awe.

The aircraft slowed, circling around the central dome of the school. It approached a landing pad on the roof of a nearby tower and gently touched down, descending into Sci Hi's underground hangar. When the elevator reached the bottom, it locked into place with a loud clang.

"You may now unbuckle your safety belts," Talos instructed from the doorway of the cockpit. "I will take you to Dr. Macron, the headmistress of Sci Hi."

Hari and Sid clambered out of their seats, grabbed their belongings, and stepped out of the aircraft into the brightly lit hangar. All around them, various aircraft were being repaired and tested. A small, spindly vehicle had transparent wings that flapped up and down, slowly at first, then so quickly they were almost invisible. The wings made a loud hum that echoed in the cavernous space. One truly titanic jet dwarfed the technicians and the robots swarming over it, making the workers look like fleas on an eagle.

Talos led them out of the hangar, up an escalator, and into the warm, breezy air outside. They walked across a small courtyard to the main building where a short elevator ride took them to Dr. Macron's office. The elevator opened in the middle of her office, which occupied the entire twentieth floor. Huge windows gave them a panoramic view of the island. Translucent panels floating around the office contained diagrams and images showing research being done around the world. Small groups of scientists huddled together, consulting on their latest findings.

"It's so good to finally have you here." A warm voice welcomed Sidney and Hari. They turned to see a tall, middle-aged woman striding across the carpeted floor. Sid recognized her from his intermaze searches on Sci Hi. She was one of the scientists who built the Beta Space Station orbiting Earth. She shook their hands firmly. "I am Dr. Macron, the Sci Hi headmistress. I wanted to meet you both before getting you squared away with your room assignments and orientation. Traditional schools may be halfway into the term, but the school year is just getting underway here."

Dr. Macron's hair was gray and tucked neatly in a bun. Her face had deep smile lines engraved on it. Her dark-green eyes were partially hidden behind dataglasses, but they sparkled with intelligence.

"I'm happy that you both took advantage of the opportunity to attend Sci Hi. I have read through your files, and I think you are exactly the type of students we look for. I can guarantee the curriculum at Sci Hi will give you opportunities to think in ways you haven't before.

"I've been a scientist my whole life. I've had the chance to work on many different projects and experiments, even working in space for a while. But this is the most exciting position I've ever held. Sci Hi is preparing the planet's next generation of scientists, engineers, and problem solvers. I hope you'll both be counted among that number." She smiled at them and said, "Here is a datacube with orientation materials, personal data that need to be completed, and a nanochip that contains a digital map of Goddard Island. You can submit the datacube to the floor proctor in your dormitory. Talos, please take Sid and Hari to the quartermaster to get settled."

"Yes, Dr. Macron." Talos's head swiveled to gaze at the boys with his glass eyes. "This way."

As the last students to arrive for the term, Hari and Sid were placed together in the Tesla dormitory. Students in the hallways glanced curiously at them as they walked by, but the boys barely noticed as they tried to take in their surroundings. The glass and steel corridors were etched with Nikola Tesla's patent drawings and plans of the electrical transformers he constructed. The Tesla building was divided into four dormitory floors. Hari and Sid's room was on the first floor, which had a large laboratory that served as a common area where students could work on projects together. All the necessary tools were built into hidden cabinets, available at the touch of a button. In the center of the room, a giant Tesla coil shot sparks into the air. A girl wearing dark protective goggles and heavy gloves adjusted a control at the base of the coil. A single bright spark snapped at the top of the coil, once every second. She smiled and waved as they walked past.

Sidney and Hari's room was small but comfortable. Beds and worktables folded out from the wall. A couple of swivel chairs and a low table were at the center of the room. There were no windows, but a large video screen showing a feed from the Mars colony covered an entire wall.

"I trust you will find everything in order," Talos said. "You may use the touch pad on the wall to contact the staff. Your floor monitor is due to arrive in approximately five minutes, thirty-two seconds."

"Thank you very much for your help," Hari said.

"Yeah, thanks," Sid said.

"My pleasure. Welcome to Sci Hi," Talos replied. The boys watched the machine smoothly turn and leave the room. As the big robot walked down the hallway, its arms rotated and retracted, its head sank down into its chest, and

caterpillar treads folded down to the floor.

"Whoa...." Sid said as the robot's new form disappeared around the corner at the end of the hall.

The boys spent a few minutes unpacking and goofing around with the video wall, looking at feeds from the far side of the moon, a space probe traveling with a comet, and a rover on Europa, Jupiter's icy moon. While Hari watched the screen, Sid started taking apart the tiny spherical remote that controlled all the room's devices. He had just pried open the cover when there was a brisk knock at the door. He looked up guiltily.

"Hi, guys," a cheerful voice said in a British accent.

A smiling girl with brown skin and jet-black hair was poking her head in the door. She wore a pair of jeans and a dark-blue Sci Hi T-shirt. "My name's Penny Day. I'm one of the assistant floor monitors. Sidney Jamison and Hari Gupta, right? Your class schedules are in the school brain, and you can access them on the wall screen like this." She touched a button at the corner of the table, and the wall screen shifted to its data voxpod mode.

Continuing her bustle, Penny brought up their schedules. "You'll be starting with Introduction to Mutations at 8:00 tomorrow morning. Your voxpods have been linked to the Sci Hi system, and they'll show you where to go. Oh, and there's plenty of information on Nikola Tesla. This building is named after him. You should read it. He was an amazing guy.

"Bathrooms and showers are down the hall. Dinner is in an hour, in the subfloor 1 cafeteria. If you need anything, my voxpod contact is T-5032-A. I think that's everything. See you guys around!" She gave them a wave as she left.

Hari and Sid were still trying to catch their breath after the Penny whirlwind when the room suddenly shook. They could hear a distant rumbling roar. On a hunch, Hari checked the school channel on the wall display, which showed an overhead view of the campus. Something was happening on the east end of the island. Several of the buildings were sinking into the ground, and a graceful aerospace vehicle was rising from an underground launch facility to ground level. As the boys watched, the engines ignited and the spacecraft lifted off into the sky, with thunderous clouds of smoky red flames trailing behind it.

Hari murmured, "Pradeep's high school doesn't have a rocket launcher."

Sidney grinned. All he could say was, "This place is lethal."

CHAPTER 4

"Class, this term we'll be discussing what mutations are and how they work." Dr. Vary, the Mutations 101 instructor, was a short, portly man with a bushy beard. He looked as if he had just stepped into class from a jungle expedition. He wore a brightly colored tropical shirt and a khaki vest with multiple pockets. Worn shorts and boots completed the look. His voice echoed in the dark lecture hall. He circled his desk at the front of the room, looking at the glittering word **MUTATION** that floated in the center of the room. As he talked, the letters morphed and grew legs, wings, and fins. Then, they zipped away.

"Before we start, let me ask a question. Who thinks mutations are a good thing?"

No one raised a hand.

"Who thinks mutations are bad?" Dr. Vary asked.

Sid was shocked when, before he could get his hand even halfway up, every hand in the class shot up. His mouth hung open in surprise. He couldn't remember a single time at Bleaker High when the entire class wanted to answer a question. He was so surprised that he still had his hand up after everyone else's went back down. Dr. Vary was looking right at him, eyebrows raised. "Do you have a question?"

"Um, no...no, sorry. I just...um, no." Sid could feel the blood warming his cheeks. *Usually, you can make it through the first week without everyone thinking you're some kind of freak*, he reminded himself. *Be cool.*

The girl sitting in front of him turned around in her chair. Sid instantly recognized Penny from his dorm building. She gave him a quick grin before facing forward again.

Sid bristled for a second, expecting a snarky remark, but her smile hadn't been mocking him. It was just a smile. *Maybe things* will *be different here*, he thought.

Dr. Vary continued his lesson. "Okay, let's take a look at how mutations have historically been shown in popular culture." Dr. Vary opened several image windows showing gigantic ants, spiders, and a praying mantis. The huge insects were terrorizing cities. People ran back and forth, screaming wildly toward the camera.

"These are scenes from films that were made during the 1950s and '60s. They showed insects that were mutated, usually by atomic radiation, and grew to be enormous. In reality, arthropods could never grow this large." Several *awwws* were heard from the class in response. "But let's leave that for a second. The reality is that mutations are simply tiny changes at the genetic level. Those changes are happening all the time, to every living organism.

"The changes happen randomly. If those changes, or adaptations, help an organism survive a new predator or a drought, then that genetic mutation is passed along to its offspring. If an organism can't survive a change to its environment, it dies, along with others of its kind, resulting in extinction. Over time, small genetic changes add up to new species. Talos, if you please...?"

The large robot moved from an alcove in the back wall to the center of the room, where a DNA strand was being projected. With a glowing fingertip, Talos reached in and moved or deleted several pieces from the coiling DNA structure. A new series of images flickered to life on the virtual screen, floating in the middle of the room. Sid squinted, absorbing the sight of tiny flies with short, crumpled wings and strangely shaped eyes. *Weird*, he thought.

"Beginning in 1910, scientists began experimenting with fruit flies to track down adaptations to specific genes. They found that radiation can cause radical mutations, which we can study and track through generations. The mutated genes are passed from parent to offspring. Talos has just altered the fruit fly's genetic string here, and the images show the resulting mutations to the fly.

"Which brings me to our term project: You will form groups of three or four to design an organism that will experience mutations, utilizing our special THING 2.0 software.

"I have created the digital world your creatures will exist in. All you will know about this world is that it has breathable air, the same gravity as Earth, and several different biomes.

"Your creatures will be inserted into the simulation. Over the term, we will see if they survive or become extinct. The team that designs the creature that survives most effectively will be announced at the Sci Hi Student Symposium at the end of the term." A hologram of the trophy appeared in an image window. "The trophy is based on a cartoon from a hard-copy publication in 1871, portraying Charles Darwin with the body of a monkey, showing the disdain his ideas were treated with during his life. We now consider Darwin's revolutionary ideas about evolution as the basis of modern biology. They have withstood scrutiny for nearly three centuries. Now it's time to see how long your creatures will last."

Sid wasn't sure how he felt about the project. He had never tried anything like it before. It sounded exciting to work on something so interesting, but he was also nervous. His specialty had always been taking things apart, not putting things together. He was worried he wouldn't be able to keep up with the other students. He leaned over to Hari. "Same team?"

Hari nodded. "Sure. We need one more. How about Penny? She seems pretty smart." He tapped her shoulder. "Penny? Do you want to work on our team?"

She turned around, flashing Hari a smile. "Cheers. That would be brilliant."

"Great," Hari said. "We can start working tonight."

The next class was Physical Education, with Ms. Newton. The students were dressed in white shorts and T-shirts covered with the Sci Hi emblem. They stood in a large gymnasium with cinder block walls and a rubber floor. Large steel beams crisscrossed the ceiling. Narrow windows spaced around the walls of the gym let in thin columns of sunlight.

"All right, everyone, listen up!" Ms. Newton shouted from the center of the gym. Her dark, spiky hair stood out in all directions. She was only a little taller than the students and wore a Sci Hi T-shirt with "Instructor" printed on the back and red sweatpants. She held what looked like a yellow soccer ball in a bulky glove on her right hand. The ball was covered with deep seams that emitted a bright blue light. "We are about to put the 'physics' into Physical Education. We're going to play a game called Zero-G Ball. It's just like dodgeball, except for one thing—the ball."

She tossed the ball into the air. Instead of falling to the floor, the ball flew up until it bounced off the gym's ceiling, then off a wall, and finally to the floor. Ms. Newton reached out with her gloved hand. The ball changed direction and stuck to the glove.

"The balls we are using for this game have been fitted with gravity nullifiers. They will continue moving until they are stopped by friction from the air, impact with the walls, or *you*.

"The motion of the ball is a perfect illustration of the property of inertia, which states that an object in motion tends to stay in motion and an object at rest will stay at rest unless an outside force acts on that object. You will be that outside force.

"The rules are the same as regular dodgeball, except you can't take someone out of the game by hitting them directly with a ball. To knock a player out, the ball must first bounce off at least one surface: a wall, the floor, or the ceiling. So, keep that in mind.

"Each team will have either red or blue balls. Let's separate into teams, with Tesla being red on that side of the gym, and Edison as blue on the other." Edison was one of the other dormitory buildings, and just as the scientists themselves were, the students in the Tesla and Edison dorms were fierce competitors.

As they took their places, the students shirts' turned red or blue. Ms. Newton tossed each side six balls, which seemed normal until the teams picked them up. Then, each ball began glowing with its team color.

A buzzer sounded, and suddenly a dozen glowing balls were bouncing around the room in every direction. The bombardment came from all sides. The shirts of those struck by an opponent's ball turned to white, and those players left the field to sit on the sidelines.

Within the first few minutes, Sid took a ball to the head. Sports had never been his thing, so he didn't mind being knocked out early and getting to watch the other players instead. Hari lasted maybe a minute longer.

They sat on the sidelines, cheering the other players on. It was hard to keep up with the crazy bouncing balls and the running, shrieking students.

Soon, there was only one player left from each team.

"That's Penny!" Hari cried.

"Yeah, she's still in the game! *C'mon Penny*," Sid shouted.

Neither Penny nor the boy on the Edison team could hit each other. Penny pitched a ball up to the rafters, way over the boy's head. Then, she started tossing balls straight at him, not fast enough to hit him, but enough to keep him in one spot. He continued to fling balls back at her.

The ball that Penny had lobbed at the ceiling bounced off it gently and hit the back wall. Everyone watching the game could see what was going to happen. The spectators jumped to their feet, shouting and calling warnings. But the Edison player was so caught up trying to hit Penny with a ball that he wasn't watching anywhere else. The ball touched the floor about three feet behind the unsuspecting

boy, bounced up slowly, and just touched his back. A buzzer sounded loudly as the Edison shirt turned white, and everyone cheered for Penny. Sid and Hari grinned, glad she was Tesla—*and* on their team.

"Now, that is a great illustration of inertia!" Ms. Newton declared.

The gravity of the balls shifted back to normal, and the balls dropped to the floor with a thud.

Penny, still elated by her victory in Zero-G Ball, led the boys to the lunchroom in the Tesla dorm. The menu was inspired by the school's international faculty and students. Hari decided on pad thai, and Penny's plate held broiled zucchini and couscous. Sid wasn't sure what he wanted to try until he spied a stack of sandwiches. "Tuna salad!" he cried excitedly, grabbing a sandwich on rye bread. He added a few pickles on the side and a large apple for dessert. He sat down with Hari and Penny and took his first bite of the sandwich. It was perfect, with just the right amount of mayo. He chewed contentedly. Sidney had no idea what the rest of his classes would be like, but at least he knew Sci Hi had tuna-salad sandwiches.

Sid's last class of the day was Microbiology. Before the class started, Talos came to the classroom to collect Hari and Sid's orientation datacubes. Hari had his ready to hand in, but Sid had only gotten through the skills and interests section. The class waited while he raced through the health questionnaire, marking the appropriate answers. For the allergies, previous conditions, and injuries boxes, he quickly selected "None," hoping he hadn't forgotten anything.

Once Sidney handed in his datacube, Talos led the class on the short walk over to a large room in the Asimov building. The sign on the door said **MINIATURIZATION**. A huge circular mirror hung from steel beams stretched across the ceiling, dominating the inside of the warehouse. The mirror was made up of thousands of tiny hexagonal lenses. Each lens had a small projector in the center of it. From below, it looked like the eye of some kind of huge insect. Mutating bugs and gravity-defying games were one thing, but Sid had a feeling that things were about to get really weird.

Technicians directed the students to climb a short flight of stairs and stand in the center of a shallow platform. A technician's voice echoed from a control room supported high above the ground by metal scaffolding, saying, "We're just going to jump right in here. I'll explain everything in a minute. But right now, eyes closed, everyone. Keep them closed until I give you the all-clear to open them again. This will help with disorientation during the miniaturization process."

Miniaturization process? Sid thought.

Suddenly, Sidney felt dizzy. His skin broke out in goose bumps, and he could feel the hairs on the back of his neck standing up. A shiver ran down his back. His fingertips felt warm, then cold, then warm again. His stomach rolled queasily, and strange colors and patterns flashed against his closed eyelids.

"All right, students. Miniaturization complete. You can open your eyes," Talos's voice boomed.

Whoa! Sidney glanced at Hari and Penny. They looked normal to him, but when he saw the mirror above, he realized what had happened. The mirror that was large when he had been normal size now looked as though it took up the whole sky. They were all nearly microscopic! A thick layer of mist was evaporating from around their feet as Sid watched.

"Pradeep *never* gets miniaturized at his school," Hari said. Sidney shook his head in agreement. He was pretty sure *no one* else ever got miniaturized at their schools.

The platform rose like an elevator. Guardrails appeared on all sides. A large, boxy structure labeled **MINIATURE RESEARCH UNIT 04** was rolled carefully next to the platform. A door in the wall slid open.

"Come in, everyone. Come in," a voice called from inside. The teacher, Dr. Sharp, was a small, thin, balding man wearing a white lab coat with the Sci Hi logo embroidered on a pocket. Sid could see jeans and a well-worn pair of hiking boots below the lab coat. Dr. Sharp had been miniaturized earlier so he could greet the students from inside the lab. "Welcome to Microbiology," he said with a grin.

The students cautiously made their way from the miniaturization platform to the research unit. Still standing on the platform, Sid couldn't take his eyes off his surroundings. At his reduced size, the steel-walled miniaturization warehouse looked as huge as the Grand Canyon.

Hari finally had to grab Sidney's arm and pull him into the research unit. "Sid, you have to see this. Come on!"

The inside of the lab was brightly lit with tiny LED bulbs that appeared as large as searchlights to the miniaturized students. The white plastic walls were smooth and shiny.

As Sid followed Hari, he came face-to-face with a honeybee the length of a city bus. The stinger was as long as Sid's hoverboard.

The bee's antenna twitched, and in a gruesome split second, it scraped against Sidney's face.

"Are you trying to kill us?" Sidney yelped. He took one last glance at the bee before running back outside. Sci Hi had been amazing, but there was no way he was up for this.

Dr. Sharp chased after Sidney. "Didn't mean to scare you, son! We just find it's better to jump right into the miniaturization process rather than try to explain it beforehand."

"Oh yeah, that. That was actually pretty cool," Sidney replied, trying to slow his heartbeat. "But I'm allergic to bees." Sidney ran his fingers through his hair, trying to shake off the feeling of the bee's antennae on his skin. "I guess I forgot...I haven't thought about that for a long time. I forgot to log it in the health datacube."

"I see. Well, then I certainly understand your reluctance to be in the same room with a huge bee!" Dr. Sharp said. "Actually, at this size, a bee sting would kill any of us. However, I assure you, there's nothing to fear. The bee has been sedated and immobilized. It can't possibly hurt you."

Sid was still doubtful, but when he stuck his head back in and looked over the bee's restraints, he felt a little better.

"Don't be shy, people, come right up and take a look," Dr. Sharp said, placing a reassuring hand on Sidney's shoulder as they slowly moved back into the lab.

Hari edged closer to the bee, reaching out a tentative finger to touch one of the spiky hairs that extended from its exoskeleton. "Wow. It feels like wire," he said.

The rest of the students crowded closer, touching the bee and watching its abdomen expand and contract.

A student raised her hand. "How come you had to miniaturize us to do this? Why couldn't you make the bee bigger?"

"That's a good question," Dr. Sharp replied. "Insects have an exoskeleton on the outside of their bodies, unlike the endoskeleton we have on the inside of our bodies. When you're very small, an exoskeleton works very well, but as you get bigger, the muscle attachments just aren't able to exert the kind of force a gigantic insect would need in order to move or even to support its own body. Another thing preventing giant insects is their lack of lungs. When they are small, they get all the air they need through diffusion. Enough air molecules actually wander into their bodies without it having to breathe as we do. Instead, air enters through holes in their sides called *spiracles*. But a huge insect wouldn't be able to take in enough air to survive."

Penny patted Sid's shoulder. "Are you all right?" she whispered.

He nodded, embarrassed by his reaction to the bee. "I was stung once when I was a little kid, and I had to be rushed to the hospital. I broke out in hives, and my throat started closing up. It was pretty scary."

"That's awful," Penny said.

"I never really think about it now, but that huge bee caught me by surprise."

"I think you could say we were all caught by surprise," Hari said ruefully.

"The reason I had us all meet here is because I wanted to discuss a very exciting research opportunity that has been presented to Sci Hi," Dr. Sharp continued. "Over the last fifty years, there has been a serious decline in honeybee populations around the world. The decline was first noticed about a hundred years ago in the early twenty-first century, and it has been growing worse. The honeybee decline could lead to catastrophic effects around the world. Worker bees responsible for caring for the young, foraging, and defending the hive are disappearing for an unknown reason. Without the worker bees, hives are dying. Scientists call the phenomenon colony collapse disorder—or CCD."

A boy raised his hand. "What's the big deal? They're just bees."

"An excellent question. Let's think about that for a moment. What do bees do?"

Penny raised her hand enthusiastically. "They gather pollen from flowers." Sid was annoyed with himself for not getting his hand up more quickly that time. *I knew that one*, he thought.

"That's correct," Dr. Sharp said. "Bees forage for food outside the nest, gathering pollen and nectar from flowers to feed the hive. One aspect of the pollen collection is very important to us humans. As they collect pollen from different plants, bees are also dropping pollen grains into those plants, enabling them to reproduce and grow. We use bees to pollinate our food crops, such as fruits and vegetables. So, tell me, what would happen to us if the little organisms we depend on to pollinate our plants become extinct?"

The students looked at one another.

"We'd starve," someone said quietly.

"Exactly," Dr. Sharp said, nodding. "Humans are dependent on thousands of other creatures, many of them considered unimportant until you understand how they impact our lives every day. So it is in our own best interests to find out what is affecting the bees before the effects become disastrous for them and for us." As he spoke, Dr. Sharp climbed a stepladder next to the bee's thorax and pointed to an orange disk stuck to its back. "Most scientists think there are many factors behind CCD. Hornets have always been a threat. But there are new factors at work as well. This orange creature is a varroa mite. It feeds on the bee's blood, which weakens the bee. It also passes diseases, such as deformed wing virus, to the bee. There are several other natural parasites, viruses, and fungi that may contribute to CCD. And around the world, humans appear to play an alarming role in hive destruction. The chemical pesticides we use and the way beekeepers move bees from field to field may contribute to the disorder."

Sid started to wonder if maybe the bees had more to fear from humans than he did from bees.

Dr. Sharp continued, "Sci Hi has been invited to research CCD at several locations around the world, and we are taking along our first-year microbiology students for a closer look. You'll all be miniaturized and allowed to conduct studies inside a living beehive alongside your instructors. You'll be notified which location you'll be assigned to shortly. At the end of the term, each team will present their findings at the Sci Hi Student Symposium."

Sid grinned at the news. "Wow!" Hari smiled back.

Penny was giddy with excitement at the chance to go inside a beehive. "That's going to be brilliant!" Her eyes sparkled. "Can you imagine? Going inside the hive with the bees still there! That'll be amazing!"

"My throat's swelling up just thinking about it," Sid said dryly.

CHAPTER 5

"Scientists don't just do their work sitting at desks," Ms. Newton explained to the students back at the main campus. "You might end up doing research in the Amazon rain forest, the Arctic Circle, or underground in a cave. You need to be in peak physical condition to do that."

The students had been training to move around inside a beehive by rock climbing. They had already learned some of the basic handholds, and now they were putting that knowledge to good use on a huge climbing wall in the cavernous gymnasium.

Ms. Newton typed a few parameters into her voxpod, and the climbing wall folded into a grade 2 climb marked with deep crevices and small ledges.

"How sure are you these zero-G harnesses will work if we fall?" Hari was slowly moving his right hand to a new handhold on the climbing wall.

"Pretty sure, I think. Try not to look down, Hari," Sid puffed as he climbed a little higher.

"You two climb like little old ladies," Penny said from near the top of the rock.

"Oh, yeah?" Sid shot back panting. "Watch this!" He tried to reach a distant handhold, but his foot slipped, and he tumbled back from the rock face into the air.

As soon as he started to fall, his zero-G harness nullified the gravity around him, and he floated gently across the gym, about fifteen feet off the ground. There were already thirty other students in the same predicament.

"Oh, come on!" Sid shouted, exasperated as he floated midair, tumbling slowly.

Just then, Hari fell away from the wall and started floating. Penny was the first one to make it all the way up the wall. She gave a victorious whoop.

"I can see that most of you need a little more practice climbing," Ms. Newton said laughing. She turned the master control for everyone's zero-G belts up a fraction, and the floating students slowly settled to the ground.

"Let's try that again," she said, and the students groaned as they struggled to their feet.

A few days later, the students were ready to experience the interior of a beehive. They put on coolsuits, which kept them comfortable inside the hive, where temperatures soared. They reminded Sidney of lightweight wetsuits, only with small cooling units on the belts. The helmets had wide acrylic faceplates and powerful lights mounted on top. Tiny cameras would record their movements, and a microphone and speakers kept them in contact with the other students and instructors.

Penny, Sid, and Hari walked with their class to the miniaturization platform. Soon, it was their turn. Sid felt dizzy for a few seconds as the miniaturizer was activated, and he wondered if he would ever get used to the feeling. Somehow, it had been easier when he hadn't known that he was about to be miniaturized. *Okay*, he told himself. *Get a grip. You can do this. There's nothing to be afraid of. You've just been miniaturized, and you're going to go into a hive of huge bees. No big deal.*

One sting would... No. That wasn't helping. He shook his head and tried to concentrate on not freaking out.

Inside the research room, there was a huge beehive anchored to the center of the floor. To the miniaturized students, it was as big as an office building.

Dr. Sharp called for everyone's attention. "All right, everyone! You'll find a scan of the hive's interior downloaded in your helmets. Use it to find your way around inside. The scan can be projected on your faceplate, using the keypad on your left arm. Make sure your gravity controls are set for wall proximity, just like in practice.

"This hive was found locally. There aren't any live bees inside, but be aware that there may be thousands of dead bees and larvae. Once inside, look for signs that the hive may have suffered from CCD."

The students started entering the hive single file. Their helmet lights switched on automatically as they crossed the threshold into the dark hive interior. Sid looked up nervously to see rows of hexagonal cells stretching into the darkness beyond the reach of his helmet light. He felt the familiar itch of curiosity take hold, crowding out his fear. He wondered what the hive must have been like when it was filled with thousands of bees coming and going. Now, it felt deserted and empty, like an old house after everyone had moved away.

"Come on, guys! Let's go," Penny said excitedly. She stepped up onto the wall of a cell the size of her body and clambered upward.

Hari and Sid followed.

"Am I crazy, or is this easier than the climbing wall in the gym?" Sid asked.

"Maybe it's because we've been miniaturized," Hari said.

They heard a yelp from Penny.

When they reached her, she was kneeling on a honeycomb shelf. Several dead bees, each the size of a small car, lay nearby, exoskeletons dull under the light of the helmets. The three friends leaned in to study the bee carcasses, looking for any sign of sickness or damage.

When Penny moved to examine another bee, Sid spotted something orange on her back. "Wait, Penny. You've got something stuck to you." He stepped past a dead bee and pulled at something attached to her respiration unit.

"Whatever this is, it's hard to get off," Sid grunted, pulling at the object.

It finally came away, stubby legs wriggling.

"It's one of those varroa mites," Hari said. "Ugh."

Penny shuddered when she turned around and saw it. "That thing's disgusting! Get rid of it."

"I think he's kinda cute," Sid said, examining it. "Look at all those little legs. He's like a fat little spider."

"Those things feed on blood! They can cut through a bee. You think they'll have any trouble cutting through our suits?" Penny retorted.

"You should get rid of it," Hari agreed.

Sid imagined the little mite slicing through his coolsuit to feed on his blood. "Maybe he's not that cute after all." He placed the mite a safe distance away in an empty cell.

The class spent several hours exploring the hive while looking for other signs of disease that might have affected the bees. Then, they reported their findings to Dr. Vary, who keyed the information into his master data log.

"Well done, everyone. I'll tabulate this information and share it during our next class. Let's move back to the miniaturizing platform so we can all get back to normal size. Then, you're dismissed."

Sid breathed a sigh of relief. He had actually spent a day inside a beehive without getting killed—or looking like an idiot.

After dinner that night, Sid, Hari, and Penny did some work designing their creature for the Great Mutation Challenge. "How about a name for our team?" Hari asked. After each suggested some names, they decided to name their team Biopocalypse because they hoped, if they made it sufficiently dangerous, their creature would dominate everything else in the simulation.

"I want to make a carnivore," Sid said as they sat down to work.

"Forget it. Carnivores need a lot of space and lots of prey to feed on," Hari said. "Very inefficient organisms."

"How about a plant eater? They're pretty tough, right?" Penny asked.

"Until a drought hits or some climate change kills off all their food," Sid said.

"Hey, what if we do something a little different?" Hari's eyes shined. "Looking at that varroa mite earlier gave me an idea. Let's try something that will be able to live through any environmental changes. Like a parasite."

"Ewww," Penny said.

"That is a totally lethal idea!" Sid sat up in his chair. "Think about it. The parasite could live on blood from any creature that has blood. That way, if one species dies out, the parasite can still find food. We could have it live inside the host's body so it's protected from outside weather. And we could program it to follow really simple rules like 'Drink blood, but not so much blood that the host dies.' I think that could really work! We'll have to think of a really gross way for it to spread. Something to do with eyeballs."

"Maybe it could take over the host's brain, controlling it like a zombie," Hari said.

"You two are absolutely sick—" Penny began, but she was interrupted by the chiming of their voxpods. "That could be our field-trip assignment!" They consulted their voxpods and saw they all were being sent to Japan to study a beehive.

"Awesome!" Sid said.

"We have to get our virtual organism designed and turned in before we go, so let's crack on," Penny reminded them. "Dr. Vary is going to let the simulation run while we're gone." She sighed. "All right, I do think a parasite is a good idea."

"*Lethal!*" Sid cried.

For the trip to Japan, the students were transported in one of Sci Hi's gigantic flying labs equipped with a miniaturizing unit and a collection of instruments needed to conduct research in remote locations. The passengers sat high up over the nose, leaving most of the fuselage free to act as a mobile laboratory.

When the jet's massive engines fired up, a cloud of dust blasted up around the plane. As the large aircraft lifted straight up from the landing pad, Sid watched the ground fall away. He could feel the thrust from the engines increasing as the jet picked up speed, rising faster and faster.

The cabin intercom interrupted Sid's thoughts.

"This is Talos, your pilot. We have reached our travel altitude of sixty-five thousand feet and will switch to scramjet engines in approximately thirty seconds. Please stay fastened in your seats at this time. Our flight will take us to the island of Tsushima, off the coast of Japan's mainland. Our flight time will be approximately five hours. Thank you."

"Hey, Talos is a pretty talented 'bot," Sid said, turning to Hari only to find he had fallen asleep with his head resting on a scratchy blanket.

Sid was restless and nervous about the trip. He hadn't done much traveling before, and now here he was zooming around the world. Even though he had only been at Sci Hi for a short time, his life had become very different. How could Hari sleep?

He turned to Penny, who was sitting on the other side of him, doing something with her voxpod. As she used a stylus on the fold-down table, lines appeared, projected by the voxpod.

"What are you working on, Penny?"

"Just doing some drawing," she replied absentmindedly, never taking her eyes from the little table where her sketchy lines were beginning to take shape.

Sid craned his neck to get a look at what she was drawing. "Really? I didn't know you like to…wow, that's great! It's a honeybee, right? How come you don't want to be an artist?"

"Scientists use art all the time to illustrate things so other people can understand them. You know, diagrams and restorations and stuff."

"How'd you learn to draw like that?" Sid asked.

"Lots and lots of drawing. That's the only way to get better. Everyone in my family is an artist of some type," Penny sighed. "Mum's a painter, my dad plays piano, my brother sculpts, and my sister wants to be an architect."

"What do they think of you wanting to be a scientist?" Sid asked.

Penny clenched her jaw. "They don't get it at all, actually. They think science has no soul, and they're disappointed that I don't want to be an artist. They were tolerant enough to let me attend Sci Hi, thank goodness. I just can't explain to them what I like so much about science. I want to *know* things. Nothing against art and music, but they don't deal with facts. Art is subjective. The same painting can mean totally different things to different people. Science is creative, too, but it's all about facts backed up by evidence, and it can change when new information is discovered. I want to find answers to questions about the universe. And I like the idea of helping people through science. I mean, really, think about what we're on our way to do. We're going to be miniaturized and enter a beehive with live bees! We might be able to help the bees survive and save our crops. That's amazing!" She shook her head. "What about you, Sid?"

"I just like taking things apart to see how they work. I guess I get that from my grandfather. He was an engineer for a toy company. One of the things he showed me was that you can understand how most things work by taking them apart. Once you understand how they work, you can make them work better, even things like buildings, and robots and spaceships. We took lots of things apart, not just toys, but bigger things like impulse ovens and micro refrigerator units when I was older. He was always able to rebuild stuff because he took his time and was careful about keeping things in order. I've gotten pretty good at taking things apart, but I'm not so good at the reassembly part yet." He sighed, "My mom has always been awesome about not killing me when I've taken apart something important. She's been great, really. I don't think I ever told her that."

They swapped stories about their families until the huge flying lab descended in a cloud of exhaust onto the makeshift landing pad of Tsushima Island. Dr. Sharp and the assistant instructors herded everyone off the jet to a camp where dome tents and long picnic tables had been set up for them.

After an informal dinner, Dr. Sharp quieted everyone for a briefing on what they would be doing over the next three days. "Welcome to Tsushima Island, everyone! Now, we know what our research is about. There has been a resurgence of colony collapse disorder in beehives around the world, and we're looking for causes.

"We're here in Japan because Japanese bees don't succumb to CCD. The first question is why not? Is there a behavioral or a biological factor that allows Asian honeybees to fend off what is killing millions of other bees? Or is it something in the Asian bees' environment that is helping them resist the various diseases and parasites we think contribute to CCD? Hopefully, we will be able to gather some hard evidence that shows how the Japanese bees are surviving when North American and European bees are dying off. That's the best way to test the theories currently being discussed.

"We know honeybees are social insects—that is, they live together in large groups. Studies have shown that bees have sophisticated methods of communication. For example, they engage in the waggle dance to direct other bees to food sources. They may even resort to head-butting a dancing bee if they think their own food source is a better one.

"A single bee may not be very intelligent, but when they work together, the hive mind can accomplish remarkable things. Simple rules like 'vibrate rapidly when threatened' can produce complex behaviors. Bees can defend their territory, vote on where to live, figure out how many workers to send out to collect pollen, and repair a hive. No bee sees the whole picture. No bee tells the other bees what to do. Each bee simply reacts to what's near it and follows the instincts that rule its behaviors.

"We may consider ourselves more intelligent than bees, but when provoked, we humans still react instinctively. We display our own version of swarming whenever an orderly crowd of people is transformed into an unruly mob. Humans use a lot more information than bees do to make decisions, but we've actually learned a lot from this form of swarm intelligence. In fact, the nanobots we use for construction projects are designed to use swarm intelligence. They are programmed with the specs of the project and provided with the raw materials. Each bot has certain rules it must follow, based on what other nearby nanobots are doing. The result is that the nanobots divide up the labor themselves and create the structure. In effect, they act as a sort of swarm."

Sidney pictured the bridge being built near his house. Warm memories of Philly lingered as he listened to Dr. Sharp continue. "All right, everyone. That's enough for tonight. Let's get some sleep. We have a busy few days ahead of us!" Dr. Sharp finished by sending the kids to their cots for the night.

Dr. Sharp's discussion left Sid's head swarming with ideas. Bees were just little insects. How could they work together to build their hives, forage for food, and then tell the other bees where that food was all without being able to speak? It took Sidney hours to fall asleep. When he did, he dreamed he was flying, skimming effortlessly over the surface of a strange world covered in huge, crumbling buildings made of gray, cracked cement. Each building had small, dark windows. When he glided closer to inspect a building, he was startled as concrete arms reached out of the windows and grabbed him. He tried to veer away, but the arms followed, stretching to follow him as he shot upward into the sky. They caught hold of his feet, slowing him down. He could feel his feet turning to stone. Tendrils of cold stone climbed his legs. He could feel himself turning gray as it spread. A rapidly spinning globe of light appeared, hanging just out of reach. He somehow knew that if he reached the light, he could escape, but he was being steadily pulled back to the gray world waiting to gulp him down like quicksand. Just as he was about to hit the ground, he woke up.

Hari was shaking him awake.

"Sid, wake up. We have to get moving. Time to be a bee!"

CHAPTER 6

With the sun up, it was time to start exploring their first live hive. A small electric vehicle towed a portable miniaturizer from the flying lab out to the hive. Dr. Sharp and Verge, one of his assistants, went first. The students followed. Sid watched as the beam projector was fired and a cloud of mist enfolded Hari and Penny. He could just make out the shrinking forms of his two friends for a moment before they seemed to disappear. The mist cleared, and then he was next on the platform.

Sid barely had time to worry if he was ready when the technician fired up the miniaturizer. When the mist cleared, he was looking at the tech's shoes, which were now the size of houses.

"Come along! Quickly! The miniaturizer platform must be cleared before the next students can be reduced." Dr. Sharp was waving them toward the microshelter. Once all the students were inside, the professor made sure everyone was strapped to the padded floor. He then signaled they were ready to be moved by flashing a series of lights. At their tiny size, his voice couldn't be heard by the assistants' normal-sized ears. When the tech detected the tiny green lights flashing on the outside of the microshelter, he gingerly lifted the box. To the microstudents inside, it felt as if the room were rocketing upward. They shrieked as the room tossed and turned. After a few brief seconds, the microshelter was fastened securely to the tree where the nest was located.

Dr. Sharp called out, "You may now unbuckle your safety harness and stand. We're going to get right to work. The coolsuits and equipment have already been miniaturized. You'll find them in the lockers against the wall. Put them on, and then Verge will spray you with a pheromone that will make you smell like a bee—well, at least to other bees. Smoke is being pumped into the hive, so the bees should be calm and docile. But don't worry, it won't have any lasting effect on the bees."

Once they were dressed, the students lined up to be sprayed.

"How do you know this stuff works?" Sid asked Verge when it was his turn.

"We located the queen and took a sample of the chemicals she normally secretes into the hive," Verge said. "Then, we mixed up a batch for ourselves. We'll all be royalty today," he said with a wink. He patted a cylinder standing beside him. "I tested it earlier, and the bees accepted it. Nothing to worry about. Okay, helmet on, please."

Once Sid was sprayed, he joined the other students standing around the entrance to the hive.

"All right! Here we go. Take your time, and try not to make any sudden moves," Dr. Sharp advised. "The bees you see will be in a somewhat sedated state, but try not to startle them. You have the shock prods so you can give the bees a mild shock if they get too curious. At this voltage, no harm will be done, but the bees will be startled enough to move away." Dr. Sharp activated his shock prod. The small metal ball on the end lit up with a halo of static electricity. He climbed up into the hive. Verge went next.

The students stood watching uncertainly until Penny said, "I don't know about you, but I'm dying to see what it's like in there! We'll be surrounded by thousands of live bees!" She ducked inside the hive and glanced back at Sid and Hari. "C'mon, don't just stand there!"

Hari started toward the hive and pulled Sid along.

As Sid poked his head into the hive interior, his helmet light came on. Dozens of lights bounced in the shadows of the cells as the class spread out to explore. The dark silhouettes of the bees could be seen on the walls. Most were resting quietly in the haze of the smoke. Some were moving hesitantly.

One bee came near Sid, touching him briefly with its antenna as it moved past.

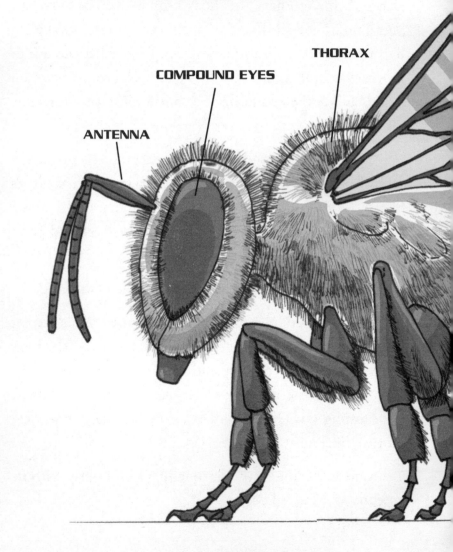

ANATOMY OF A HONEYBEE
CLASSIFICATION: APIS MELLIFERA
MAGNIFICATION: 20X

THORAX

COMPOUND EYES

ANTENNA

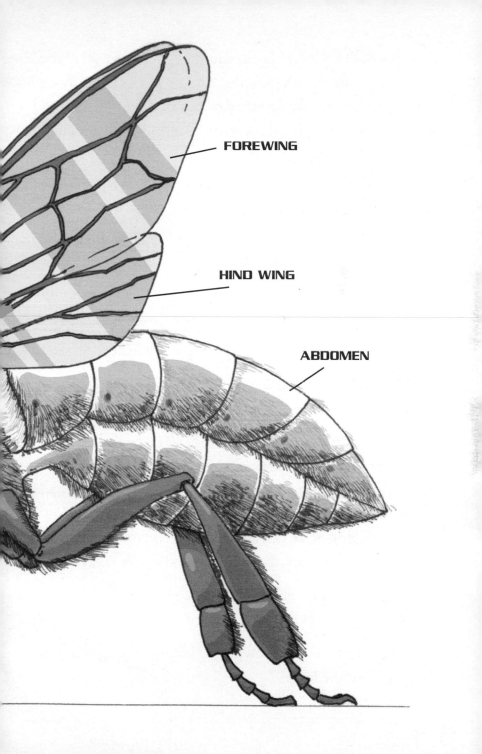

FOREWING

HIND WING

ABDOMEN

Startled, Sid jerked back, slamming into the wall of the hive. Expecting the bee to sting him, he grabbed the shock prod from his belt and activated it. But the bee only stopped for a moment, regarding him with its unreadable compound eyes before continuing on its way.

After that first relatively uneventful contact, Sid felt more at ease moving through the hive. The bees didn't seem to take the slightest notice of him with his much smaller size and the queen's familiar scent.

"Sid, what's taking you so long?" Hari called from up ahead. "Are you all right?"

"I'm fine," he replied. "Right behind you."

The cells built into the walls of the hive made for easy climbing. There were plenty of secure footholds.

This hive is amazing, Sid thought. *How could they build something like this without plans? They can't even talk to each other.* After his sting when he was younger, Sidney had always been afraid of bees. But now that he could study them more closely, he was able to keep a lid on his fear and focus on how amazing and interesting the bees really were.

Sid looked up and saw he was approaching the ledge where Penny had stopped. She waved.

"Good to see you, slowpokes," Penny said as Sid and Hari reached the ledge.

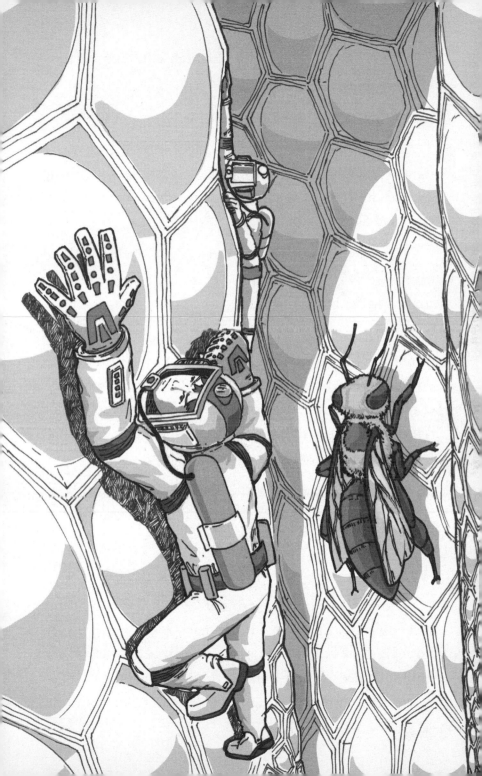

"Very funny," Hari said. "Enough climbing for me." He cast his helmet light into the dark.

"Me, too," Sid panted. "I must be *really* out of shape."

"Guess we can stop climbing and start exploring what's right here," Penny said. She set out along the ledge, starting a visual check of the bees that were hanging on to the walls. Hari and Sid followed her.

"I'm not seeing mites," Hari said. "That seems kind of strange. We saw so many of them in the dead hive we studied in Sci Hi, remember?"

"Yeah. You're right," Sid said. He turned up the cooling system for his suit. Beads of sweat were rolling down his neck. He was breathing hard. It felt as if he were still climbing vertically, but now he was simply walking along a flat shelf jutting out from the hive wall. He glanced over at Hari, but he didn't seem to be struggling.

"Hari, Sid, can you shine your lights inside this cell? I want to see if there are any mites on the larvae," Penny asked.

"Sure," Hari said as he joined her.

Sid started to move, too, but he was struck suddenly with a wave of dizziness. His stomach rolled unpleasantly. Struggling to keep his balance, he grabbed a cell in the wall and tried to stop himself from falling off the ledge. A red light started blinking inside his suit helmet, and the

faceplate lit up with an infographic of the coolsuit's systems. The breathing unit was failing!

Sid tried to call out to Hari and Penny, but he was panting too hard to get out the words.

He felt panic start to invade his mind. He knew he had to get outside and take the helmet off immediately. But when Sidney tried to move, he had trouble commanding his legs. Instead of walking, all he could do was sink down to his knees and lean back against the hive wall.

"Heh—heh— help…." he groaned weakly.

Penny watched him sink to the ground. "Sid, what is it? What's wrong? Have you…have you been *stung*? Hari, help me! Something's wrong with Sid!"

Sid couldn't answer. He felt as if a curtain were closing across his mind. He was having trouble thinking straight. Suddenly, he felt a tug under his arms, and he was yanked off the ledge as Penny and Hari cranked up their gravity nullifiers and jumped. Within seconds, they were on the floor of the hive, where they found Dr. Sharp and Verge, who helped get Sid outside. They quickly removed his helmet.

The warm, fuzzy feeling in Sid's head that had been getting worse was suddenly wiped away. His thoughts crystallized back into focus. He could breathe again.

"What…what happened?" he asked.

"Nothing to worry about, my boy," Dr. Sharp said. "Although you gave us a bit of a scare for a moment there."

"Something damaged your regulator," Verge said. "Did something hit you in the back? The rebreather unit is dented."

"No, I don't think so. Wait. I did back into the hive wall when a bee came past me."

"That might have done it. Well, your vitals are looking better now," Verge said, looking at the small screen built into the left forearm of the coolsuit.

Dr. Sharp said, "Let's not take any chances. I'll beam these readings back to Dr. Pritchard to get her opinion. Verge, round up the students. I think we've been in the hive long enough for today. We'll start our three-day excursion tomorrow." Verge nodded as he fastened his helmet and strode toward the hive.

"How do you feel, Sidney?" Dr. Sharp asked.

Penny and Hari helped Sid sit up. "Okay, I guess," he said cautiously.

"You certainly look better," Penny said.

"You were turning blue when we got you out here," Hari added.

"I don't think I want to go through *that* ever again," Sid said emphatically.

"I can imagine," Dr. Sharp replied. "Let's get you back to the shelter and out of that coolsuit. I'll replace the rebreather unit after we eat."

Hari and Penny helped Sid make it to the shelter. By the time they reached it, he was feeling back to normal.

During dinner, Dr. Sharp read off some of the statistical data the students had collected in the hive. Temperature and humidity were normal. The population of the hive was normal. The proportion of young to old workers was within normal limits. Their brief visit to the hive hadn't yet uncovered any obvious reason why Japanese honeybees didn't seem to suffer from colony collapse disorder.

After everyone had finished eating, the students were free to hang out in the microshelter lounge. They clustered by the windows, mesmerized by the now giant world outside. House-size mushrooms grew on tree bark that wrinkled and folded like a mountain range. A caterpillar the size of a tanker truck crawled over the microshelter while a hummingbird hummed like a helicopter as it darted past.

Penny could tell Sid was still shaken by his rebreather accident, so she tried to give him something a little less stressful to talk about.

"What would you be doing if you were back home?" Penny asked as she leaned against a giant cushion cut from a block of foam.

"It's almost winter there, so I'd probably just be hibernating, watching movies, and looking for stuff to take apart. What about you, Penny? You're from London, right?"

Penny nodded. "My favorite hangout is the Natural History Museum in London. It was the first of its kind in the world. I live near a lot of museums. What about you, Hari?"

"In the winter, I'd be drinking chai and telling stories with my family around the fire. In the summer, it gets really hot in Delhi—about forty-six degrees in July," Hari said.

"That doesn't sound hot to me," Sid said.

Hari's eyebrows shot up, and then he laughed. "Forty-six degrees *Centigrade*. That's about one hundred and fifteen degrees Fahrenheit."

Penny whistled. "That *is* a bit on the warm side."

"So what is it you guys want to do, once you're done with high school and college and everything?" Sid asked.

Penny replied, "I'm interested in biotech—nanomachines as small as cells, things like that. Really amazing stuff. I want to be part doctor and part engineer. I think it will be brilliant. What about you, Hari?"

"Something to do with space exploration and astronomy," Hari mused. "I'd love to build one of those space probes that travel to other planets or listen for signals from aliens."

"I want to take things apart," Sid said. "I don't know if there are any jobs like that, but I think that would be fun. Kind of like being a 'reverse engineer.' I'd take things apart and then put them back together so they worked even better than before. If I can't take things apart, I think robots are pretty awesome. I wouldn't mind taking Talos apart to see how he works."

"Not that he'd let you," Penny laughed.

Before long, it was time to go to sleep. The next day would be spent entirely inside the hive, probing its secrets.

The next morning, the students reentered the smoky hive. The class was buzzing with excitement. Sid, Hari, and Penny worked together, climbing the honey-laced cells past hundreds of worker bees. Honey oozed and dripped from some of the cells. They set out to record the number of bees they encountered, the condition of the pupae, and the temperature of the air at different locations throughout the hive.

As Sid climbed the cells, he spotted some movement a little way up the vertical wall of cells. He squinted, trying to make out what was happening in the light cast by his helmet lamp.

"Hey. Hey, guys, look at this!" Sidney climbed higher to see better. It looked like the worker bee was removing a pupa from its cell. Something was wrong, though. The pupa was still a translucent white color, with its six legs folded tightly against its body. It was much too young to leave the cell.

Penny and Hari joined Sid. They watched as the pale, unmoving pupa was pulled from its cell.

"Look!" Hari pointed at several small, orange clusters attached to the pupa. "Those look like varroa mites!"

The bee clumsily dropped the pupa to the floor of the hive and climbed down after it.

"What the heck is it doing?" Sid tried to make out the bee, but it was lost in the darkness. "I can't see."

"Night vision," Hari reminded him. "Third button on your right arm." "Quick, let's follow it!" Penny clambered down the hive wall.

Sid touched the button. His faceplate glowed with a ghostly green light, showing details of the hive. "Lethal!" Sid said. He hurried after Hari and Penny.

They clambered down the cells of the hive, dodging sluggish workers and the occasional drone. Other students turned to watch them descend.

"Is anything wrong?" Dr. Sharp's voice crackled in their helmets.

"Penny here. I think we're onto something, Dr. Sharp," Penny said over the suitcom. "We're following a worker that dragged a pupa from one of the cells. It seems to be moving down toward the hive entrance."

"Interesting," Dr. Sharp replied. "I'm patching into your video feed now. Keep following it if you can."

Sid and Hari reached the floor of the hive and scrambled to follow Penny. Soon, they arrived at the hive entrance. The light from the outside world was almost too bright for them to bear after the hive's cavernous darkness.

"There! It's over there," Penny pointed to a bee that had ventured onto the microshelter platform bolted to the hive. They hurried over just in time to see the bee dump the mite-infested pupa over the side before turning and making its way back to the hive.

"Whoa!" Sid said, peering over the edge of the platform to the ground, far below. "That bee just dumped that thing like it was trash."

"Fascinating," Dr. Sharp said as he emerged from the hive. "What do you think might be the reason for the bee's behavior?"

Hari frowned. "Maybe it didn't want the mites to spread to any of the other bees?"

"That's my thought, too," Dr. Sharp said. "The life cycle of varroa mites starts with young mites feeding on the immature bee, but once the bee matures, so do the mites. They spread to other bees and lay eggs in other cells with immature bees. Once they're in, they can quickly spread through the hive. They also spread diseases to the bees as they feed on their hemolymph, which is similar to our blood. That weakens the bees.

"Perhaps the bees in this hive have a gene that results in the behavior we have just witnessed. When pupae infested with the mites are recognized in the hive, they are removed. This cuts down on the spread and growth of the mites in the hive. Your finding may have given us an opportunity to conduct an experiment. If we were to mark those pupae that are infested with mites and take some chemical samples, we might be able to track down the factors that make the bees eject them from the hive. It could be a visual cue, or some scent the bees are able to detect. We'll share the video and talk about that with the other students tonight," Dr. Sharp concluded.

Sidney felt a rush of pride. He knew they had been lucky to be in the right place at the right time. But if they hadn't watched closely, they might have missed making an important discovery.

The remainder of the day passed uneventfully. The students were given the option of sleeping in the microshelter or camping in the hive for the night.

Sid and Hari were undecided, but Penny convinced them to spend the night inside the hive. "It's a once-in-a-lifetime chance! How can you pass it up?" Her enthusiasm was contagious.

"Okay, count me in," Hari relented. "I'm pretty sure Pradeep's never spent the night in a beehive."

"What happens if the pheromone stuff wears off in the middle of the night?" Sid asked. "I don't want to wake up to a mad bee attack."

Hari thought for a second. "Well, they must have tested it before they let us stay the night, don't you think?"

Penny sighed, exasperated. "You two worry way too much. Everything's going to be fine."

"Okay, but if you get stung to death or ripped apart by bee mandibles, don't come crying to me," Sid muttered.

Sleeping harnesses were attached to the hive wall in the same way mountain climbers attach themselves to the side of a cliff during overnight climbs. Sid didn't think it would be comfortable, but once he deployed his hammock, his exhaustion from the long day caught up with him. The drone of his respirator synced with the bees' buzzing, and the sound lulled him to sleep. He dreamed of honey as Dr. Sharp stayed up to review the footage of the bee dumping the infected pupa.

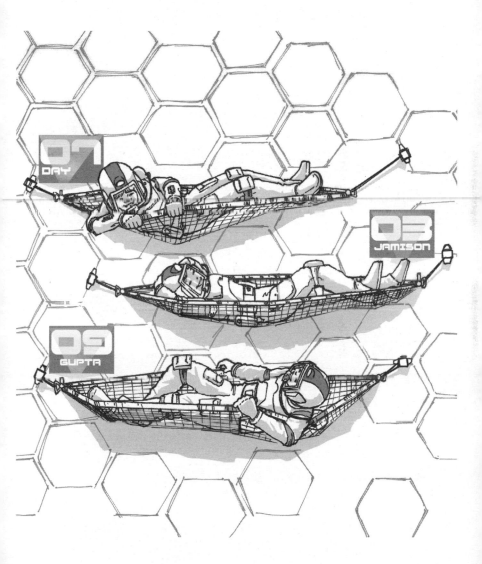

CHAPTER 7

The next morning, Penny, Hari, and Sidney returned to the microshelter for breakfast. The other students lined the long tables set up for them, eating and chatting about the exciting day to come. Sid wolfed down another protein bar. Even in his micro state, his appetite was as big as ever. As he ate, he inspected one of the shock prods used to electrocute any bees that got too curious. The mental itch of his curiosity was focused on how the shock prods worked. And the only way to scratch that itch was to take something apart. He cracked open the titanium casing and stared at the inside.

"What's up?" Hari asked, sitting down with a tray of food.

"Nothing!" Sid replied guiltily, but when he saw the grin on Hari's face he relaxed. "Habit, I guess. You know, I think I could make these things deliver a *really* big shock if I reversed the polarity of these two modules."

"I hope you disconnected the battery before you started poking around in that thing," Hari said. "Otherwise, *you'll* be the one getting the really big shock."

Sid flashed him a look of annoyance. "Of course, I…." *Oops.* He located the power cable. It was still attached to the battery pack. "Well, I'll make sure I do it next time," he said sheepishly, disconnecting the cable.

"I wonder if our virtual parasites are surviving," Penny said. "I can't wait to see if they've spread while we've been in the hive. I really want to win! I wonder what they're doing right now."

"Well, I'll tell you what they'd *better* be doing," Sid said. "They'd better be infesting eyeballs. If I find out they were slacking off all this time, that's it. Extinction for them."

Hari put down a piece of toast dripping with jam. "Can we talk about something else, please? Eyeball parasites are not something I want to talk about while I'm eating."

Sid shrugged. "Sure, if that's what you want."

Penny was excited to spend another day in the hive. "I'm not leaving there until I see the queen," she said with determination.

"That sounds awesome," Hari agreed.

Sid wasn't excited about meeting the queen face-to-exoskeleton, but it was clear that Penny wouldn't stop until she found her. "Okay," he said. "I'm in."

After finishing their breakfasts, the three friends lined up to be sprayed with the pheromone that made them smell like the queen, and Dr. Sharp and Verge led all the students in for their second full day in the hive. The students scattered, observing the different tasks the bees performed.

"Look at this," Hari said, gesturing to a solitary bee hard at work. "I think he's making new cells."

"She," Penny corrected. "All the workers are female. Just like in real life," she added sarcastically.

"Hey! Was that a slam?" Sid retorted. "I bet there are plenty of hardworking male bees around here somewhere."

"Good luck finding one," Hari said. "They're called drones, and they're outnumbered by workers. They don't make honey, and they can't sting. Their only purpose is to mate with the queen."

"Whose side are you on?" Sid muttered.

"The workers kick them out of the hive in the fall. The poor dopes can't even feed themselves. Just like my brother," Penny said.

They watched the worker toil tirelessly, building cell after cell.

"Kind of amazing that they know how to do all this work without having to be told how, isn't it?" Sid asked, watching the worker.

"Instincts are powerful," agreed Hari.

After observing the worker bee a bit longer, Penny started making her way deeper into the hive. "Okay, time to find the queen!"

They followed along a wall that spiraled into the depths of the hive. The bees they passed still appeared tranquilized amidst the smoke that wafted like curtains in the dark space.

"We have to be pretty close to the center of the hive," Hari said. "The curve of the wall is getting tighter."

"Hey, you guys? I'm getting a little worried that we can't hear anyone else. Are you picking up a signal on your suitcom?" Sid asked. The map of the hive on his helmet faceplate was breaking up.

"I can't hear anyone, either," Hari replied. "Maybe we'd better..."

"*There she is!*" Penny shouted, pointing while she clung to the wall near a horizontal shelf of cells. "There's a huge open space down there. You've got to see this! The queen is there, and she's magnificent!"

Hari and Sid made their way over the sticky cells until they reached Penny and could look over the rim of the hive. They gasped at what they saw. The queen was at the center, and she was huge. They had almost gotten used to seeing bees the size of cars, but the queen was the size of a tanker truck. Her massive, glossy body was surrounded by workers feeding and cleaning her. She continually reassured them with touches of her antennae.

"Holy smokes, she's big," Sid whispered.

Hari just nodded.

"Come on, you two," Penny chided. "I can barely see her from here."

"Penny, I don't know if it's a good idea to get too close...." Hari began.

"Where's your sense of adventure?" she interrupted. "You can wait here if you want, but I'm going in for a closer look." She began to negotiate the hexagonal cells down to where the queen and her court were located.

Hari looked at Sid and shrugged. "Might as well. How many times in your life will you get the chance to meet a queen bee?"

"I'm going to look around for mites first," Sid said. "I'll shoot some video. Penny's so excited she'll probably forget."

"Sounds good."

"Don't make the queen mad," Sid warned as Hari moved deeper into the hive. Sidney sat on the edge of a cell and shot some video of the queen's chamber with the camera built into his helmet, scanning for the little orange mites. Then, he zoomed in to see what the giant insect looked like up close.

The queen's head was enormous next to Penny and Hari. But her head and thorax were small compared with her gigantic abdomen, which was filled with the eggs that kept the hive populated. A young worker was feeding the queen a drop of honey. Others were scattered around her, keeping the chamber clean and repairing the cell walls.

Penny walked close to the queen's head, careful not to move too quickly and startle the workers. "I bet Pradeep's never stood next to a queen bee, has he, Hari?" she said.

Hari laughed. "Nope. I'm pretty sure he hasn't."

Sid was focused on filming Penny and Hari when a quick burst of static made him jump. He used the suit's controls to home in on the frequency. He could barely make out broken voices saying something urgently.

"*Repeat! All students must...*zzt...*immediately. We have spotted giant...*zzt...*in the vicinity. These insects are extremely...*zzt...*do not approach. Evacuate the nest and...*zzt... immediately...*zzt."

Sid jumped up. "Hey. *Hey.* HEY, GUYS! Something's going on!" He could see Hari and Penny straighten up.

"What is it, Sid?" Hari asked.

"I just heard something that sounded like a...like a *warning*. It was pretty broken up, but I think we'd better get out of here and head back to the microshelter."

"Come on, Sid. You're just getting spooked," Penny said. "Just a bit longer, and we'll go."

Another broken communication came over the com channel. "*Swarm of...zzt...spotted, closing in. Arrival at the hive in...zzt...mately five minutes.*"

"Penny, we have to leave *now*!" Sid cried. "Something's coming!"

Hari spoke up. "Maybe we'd better go, Penny."

"Okay, okay," Penny said grudgingly. "I can see her again tomorrow."

As Penny and Hari climbed out of the queen's chamber, Sid was becoming more anxious. "Climb faster!"

"Oh, relax—" Penny started, but she was interrupted by another burst of communication.

"*Scouts sighted! Take shelter immediately! These...zzt... extremely dangerous! Do not approach!*"

"Whatever they're talking about, it sounds bad," Hari said. "Let's go."

They started back to the hive entrance, making their way carefully but quickly along the cells.

"Look at the bees," Penny said.

The worker bees were moving restlessly. The tranquilizing smoke had cleared, and the bees were becoming more active. They looked like they were shivering. First one bee shook, and then another, almost like fans doing the wave at a football game.

"I think they're alerting the others," Sid said.

A few minutes later, the three friends had nearly made it back outside. But they were blocked by hundreds of worker bees standing at the entrance, facing out in rows like an army.

"Something's definitely up," Sid said. "They're all waiting for something."

Just then, a huge shadow fell across Sid's face and landed on the floor of the hive.

The worker bees buzzed loudly, antennae twitching, as a huge head thrust itself into the entrance.

Penny gasped.

Sid tried to make sense of what he was seeing. It was an insect's head, similar to the bees'. But the intruder's head was gigantic, several times larger than that of the bees'. "It's a giant Asian hornet!" Hari said. "They're five times the size of the honeybees."

"So? What's going to happen?" Sid wondered. "It's huge, but there's only one. How much damage can it do?"

Hari looked at him. "If I'm remembering right, thirty of those giant hornets can wipe out a hive of thirty-thousand bees in just a few hours. The first ones that arrive are scouts. They mark the hive with a chemical to attract the others."

"What?!" Sid exclaimed. "That is totally lethal. I mean *truly* lethal."

"What do we do?" Penny asked.

Hari shook his head. "The hornets will kill the adult bees and then take the larvae and pupae back to their own hive to feed their young."

"We can't let that happen!" Penny exclaimed. "The hornets will destroy the hive! We have to do something!"

"Look at the size of that thing," Sid said. "It's absolutely mammoth. What can we do about it when we're so small?"

Another snippet of static came over the com speakers, "*Three students are still inside the hive! Zzt...can't help them now, it's too dangerous to approach the hive until...zzt...*"

"That's it, then," Sid said quietly. "We're trapped in here with those hornets unless we figure out something."

"Sid's right, Penny. We can't do anything to help them. We need to figure out how to stay alive ourselves," Hari said.

SHOCK
TERMINAL

"Wait! What about the shock prods?" Sid asked. "Maybe they'd be strong enough to at least stun those things a little."

"I don't know," Penny said. "Those prods don't look like they'd do more than tickle them."

The hornet pushed its way farther into the hive. A nearby bee attacked it. The hornet responded by catching the bee in its jaws, and with a quick chomp, bit off the bee's head.

"No!" Penny cried out.

Sid ran to the hive entrance, shoving past the guard bees. He pushed a button on his prod and a thin metal rod snapped out. The little ball on the end lit up.

INSULATED
HANDGRIPS

CONTROLS

"Sid, wait! What are you doing?" Hari called.

Sid paused at the entrance of the hive, looking into the reflective eyes of the huge hornet. In his micro state, the hornet was the size of a small airplane, and its wings hummed loudly as it moved into the hive.

The hornet's jagged jaws opened, threatening any creature that dared to stop it.

Mustering his courage, Sid jabbed the hornet's face.

A spark lit up the end of the prod, zapping the hornet. It backed up a step, more surprised than hurt. As it darted forward again, Sid stabbed it in the mandible. This time, the hornet jerked its head up, but it didn't back up.

Hari called out, "Sid, get back! These prods aren't powerful enough to stop the hornet!"

"They might not be right now, but they will be in a minute!" Sidney ran back to them, and cracked open the prod and switched the inner power regulators. "Open yours up and switch these two modules. If I'm right, they'll deliver a lot more juice." Hari and Penny scrambled to follow his lead.

Determined, Sidney watched for an opening and then lunged with his modified shock prod.

"Eat *this*!" he shouted as he swung the end of the prod at the hornet's face.

A bright flash of light flooded the hive entrance as a blinding spark of electricity leaped from the prod to the hornet's exoskeleton. A loud clap filled Sid's ears, and he was thrown backward. When he got back on his feet, the hornet was gone.

"YES!" he crowed. "It works! C'mon, you guys!" Hari and Penny waded through the bees to reach him and activated their shock prods. But when another hornet landed at the entrance, the bees reacted differently. This time, they backed away from the hornet as it pushed its way into the hive.

"What are they doing?" Hari asked nervously as he, Sid, and Penny were left alone at the entrance.

"Move back. I think the bees have something in mind," Sidney said. The three friends ducked into the cells of the honeycomb.

The giant hornet was now completely inside the hive. But rather than retreating further, the bees began to surround it. A worker bee lunged forward, closing its jaws around one of the hornet's legs. Before the hornet could open its jaws to deal with this nuisance, another worker bee attacked. Then another and another, each triggered by the last. Suddenly, hundreds of bees swarmed, containing the hornet within a vicious shell of death. The bees were vibrating rapidly. Sid toggled the controls on his faceplate and activated the thermal filter. What he saw made him gasp.

The temperature at the center of the warrior bees was much higher than on the outside. The bees continued crawling, buzzing, and vibrating their bodies. "The bees are *cooking* the hornet!" Sidney shouted. "The vibrations are creating massive amounts of heat!" After a few more moments, the bees dispersed, revealing the baked, unmoving carcass of the hornet.

"Whoa," Penny whispered. Sid and Hari nodded silently.

But there was no time to contemplate what had just happened. More of the colossal intruders were squeezing their way into the hive. As each one entered, worker bees mobbed it.

"We have to help them!" Sid said. "There aren't enough bees to go after all the hornets."

Penny agreed. "If we don't, the hornets will kill us after they're finished with the bees."

"We have to be careful. These giant hornets are dangerous to regular people. They could kill micros like us with a single bite," Hari warned.

For a fleeting moment, Sid worried about his bee allergy, then realized that at this size, Penny and Hari were in the same danger of being stung as he was. There was nothing to be done except fight. And he wasn't going to let them fight alone.

"Are we doing this or what?" Sid asked.

"Only one way out!" Hari replied.

Penny raised her prod. "Let's do this!"

Together, the three friends stood at the entrance to the hive, holding their shock prods like spears and jolting the hornets whenever they attempted to land. Their hard faces couldn't show emotion, but the hornets definitely seemed to prefer not being shocked.

Whzzap! Wild streaks of electricity crackled through the hive.

The bees bravely tried to defend their home, but more and more hornets were arriving to pillage the hive. The ground around the hive became littered with dying bees, sliced in half by the hornets' hungry mandibles. Sid, Penny, and Hari were doing their part by shocking the huge bugs, but it was clear the bees were losing even though they completely outnumbered the hornets.

"My battery's low!" Hari cried out.

Sid and Penny checked the power levels on their shock prods. Theirs, too, were almost exhausted.

Their helmet speakers crackled again, faintly. "Zzt... *approximately forty hornets sighted, but more may be on the way...zzzt...complete lockdown of microshelter! This is a Red Priority! Take shelter immediately...zzt.*"

"Forty of those huge things? The shock prods will never last long enough to scare them off!" Sid cried.

"We can't just let them die!" Penny shouted over the buzzing of the bees.

Sidney scanned the hive, taking in the gruesome insect war. They were out of options. "We have to," Sid called back. "Once these batteries run out, we've got no way to defend ourselves from those things! There's no way we can fight them, Penny. We have to get out of here, while we still have some shock power left. Now!" He grabbed Penny's arm and tried to tug her away from the insect massacre.

"Let go!" she yelled, yanking her arm free. Her brown eyes blazed in anger.

"Sid's right, Penny," Hari said quietly. "The hornets are going to win this. We have to get out before they kill all the bees and get inside the hive. We won't stand a chance against them once they're inside."

The bees were throwing themselves at the hornets, but the pile of severed bee bodies and heads just kept growing higher on the ground outside.

Finally, Penny backed away from the entrance. As soon as the trio ventured into the depths of the hive, the number of bees dropped off sharply. They had all reported to the hive entrance to fight off the hornets.

"So, where do we go?" Penny asked softly.

"Those hornets want what's inside. If we can find some way out, I think we'll be safe," Sid said. "I say we climb to the top and try to break out of the hive."

They climbed in silence, moving higher along the vertical cell walls into an older part of the hive. The cells there were worn and paper-thin, crumbling under their feet. Penny's gravity belt yanked her back from a fall when her foot punctured a cell wall.

"I don't think we can go much farther this way," Hari said. "The walls won't support our weight."

Sidney looked back. "The hornets are inside the hive. I can see them below us. They'll be coming this way soon. We either need to find a place to hide or get out of this hive right now!"

"We might be able to break through these cells," Hari said as he crumbled a piece of cell wall in his hand. He clambered inside a cell, made a fist, and punched a hole through. Honey oozed from the wall. "It works! Come on!" He started to tear at the hole he had made, making it larger. Huge gobs of honey dripped like tree sap.

"I will never eat honey again," Penny swore as she tore at the cells. Honey was dripping on their faceplates. When they tried to wipe it away, it only smeared, making the hive look yellower than ever.

Sid felt a sharp tug on his foot. He looked through the haze of honey to find himself staring into the glossy eyes of a giant hornet. The claws on its forelimb had caught on Sidney's leg. It was so close he could see the tiny hairs growing from its pitted face. His horrified expression was reflected back at him in the thing's dark, unblinking eyes. The hornet's jagged mandibles opened wide.

Sid screamed.

Hari grabbed his friend's arms and pulled, but the monster was too strong.

Penny hurled honey at the hornet's eyes, using the same precision she displayed in zero-G ball. A glob of the sticky, sweet stuff pummeled the hornet's eyes. "How do you like that, you big bully?!" she taunted.

The huge insect paused for a split second, and raised its foreleg to rub its eyes. Sidney yanked his foot free.

Hari ripped into the hive wall and scrambled through. "Let's go—while that thing can't see us!"

"I'll bet Pradeep's never fought off a giant hornet, has he?" Sid remarked with relief.

Hari grinned back at him. Penny and Sid raced after Hari as he dug through the cell walls.

"We have to be near the outer wall. Keep going," Sid said.

Finally, Hari's hand tore through the wall, and a shaft of light broke into the hive.

"We're through!" yelled Penny.

They climbed up through the last sticky layers to the top of the hive, raised their sticky faceplates, and peered down at the ground.

Thousands and thousands of dead bees surrounded the hive.

"Oh, man. What a slaughter," Sid said quietly.

"Look what those *things* have done," Penny said, shaking her head. "They came here and...and...." She raised a hand to her mouth, unable to continue.

"I really thought the bees would be able to stop them," Hari said quietly. "They outnumbered the hornets by thousands. I never imagined anything so vicious."

Sid looked at him. "I think we're lucky *we* didn't end up in that pile down there."

The giant hornets were already starting to leave, carrying the bees' larvae and pupae back to their own hive. Penny, Sid, and Hari sat despondently on top of the hive and watched as the last hornets flew back to their nest.

A voice sounded in their helmets.

"This is Dr. Sharp. The hornets have cleared the area. It is now safe to approach the hive. We need to begin searching for the missing students immediately."

"They must not know we're okay," Hari said. He activated his transmitter. "Dr. Sharp! This is Hari Gupta. I'm here with Penny Day and Sid Jamison. We're all fine!"

"Hari! Thank goodness! We were so worried. We're coming to the hive now. Sit tight and we'll have you out of there quickly...."

Sid could see several microsize humans approaching the hive's entrance. "We're up here, guys! Hey, up here!" He stood and waved his arms. One of the tiny people below waved back.

Sid sat back down next to Penny. "I'm glad that's over, aren't you, Penny? Penny, are you okay?"

She looked at him with bleak eyes, shaking her head sadly. Sidney nodded. There was nothing okay about this situation. The three friends sat quietly as they waited to tell the others what they had seen.

CHAPTER 8

After the showdown in the hive, returning to classes at Sci Hi was a welcome relief. Sid, Penny, Hari, and the other students were eager to learn the results of the Great Mutation Challenge. A few days later, Sid and Hari sat in front of the image wall, studying the data their organism had generated while they were gone.

"This can't be right," Hari said. "It can't be."

"Yeah, it can," Sid replied. "It's totally lethal! Our eyeball parasite infected almost fifty percent of the animals in the simulation! See, I told you. Eyeballs! We are going to win this, Hari, you watch. Hey, where's Penny? She's got to see this. I can't believe she didn't think the eyeball thing would work."

Sid punched in her voxpod code, and a window opened on the image wall. Penny was sitting at her desk across the room from the voxpod on her bed. Her room was decorated with the periodic table of elements on one wall and pictures and posters from her favorite band, Fusion Giraffe, on the other. "Hey, Penny!" Sidney said. "Come on over. You have to see how our parasite is doing. At this rate, all the animals' eyeballs will be infected by...hey, are you all right?"

"Fine," she said listlessly. "Just tired."

"We have to get our presentation ready for the Symposium," Hari said. "We could use your help with the animations. You're the only one of us who has any artistic talent."

Penny stared offscreen, frowning. "Okay. I'll be there in a few minutes."

Sid sat back down at his desk, pushing the pieces of a disassembled antigravity ball out of his way. "Have you noticed that Penny's been in a weird mood since we got back from the field trip?"

Hari nodded, changing the channel on the image wall to display a space probe hanging in the atmosphere of Jupiter. The thick orange clouds rushed past, hypnotizing him. "She took the hornet attack hard. She really liked the bees, and I think she was pretty shocked at the way the bee colony was wiped out. I don't blame her. It was really intense."

"Yeah, but the hornets were just being hornets, right? Being mad at them for attacking the bees is like being mad at a spider for catching a fly, or being mad at a lion for eating a gazelle. They're all just doing what they were born to do," Sid said. "We just happened to be there to see it this time, that's all." He picked up a sonic screwdriver and poked around inside the zero-G ball.

"I know you're right, but it's still hard to watch something like that happen," Hari said. "Penny just needs some time to accept it. She'll be fine."

As the term drew to a close, it was time for the Sci Hi Student Symposium. The students presented their findings on everything from microbiology to advanced intergalactic spacecraft design. A panel of world-renowned scientists and former Sci Hi students was seated in the back, ready to score each project according to how well the students followed the scientific method and yielded results that were reproducible and compelling. The large auditorium was packed with students and faculty eager to watch. Sidney had never seen a gathering like this at the schools he had attended.

The auditorium had been expanded to its full size, and a light show of the atoms colliding in the underground particle accelerator was projected on the ceiling like a fireworks display. When a particle collision made a bright flash, an "oooh" or "aahhh" could be heard from the crowd that packed the cavernous space. Flags draped along the walls of the auditorium were decorated with the faces of scientific greats from around the world and every age of civilization. Aristotle, Curie, Ibn al-Haytham, Darwin, Newton, Sagan, and Macron were all honored. Students sat in groups according to the dormitory they were housed in. As the hovering cameras projected their faces onto huge holographic screens, they cheered and waved.

Dr. Macron hosted the event with flair. She still wore her lab coat, but today it displayed animations of atomic structures making complicated patterns that changed second by second. When she stepped to the podium, a small robot floated nearby, picking up her voice and amplifying it for the other students. Her image was displayed on the center screen at the front of the room. "Hello, everyone," her voice echoed. "I truly enjoy attending these events where we share what we have learned with one another. Presenting our observations is one of the most crucial aspects of the scientific method. Every scientist is expected to present evidence, observations, and experimental results to other scientists, whether through a publication, a symposium, or a meeting like this one. This process allows the scientists' data and methods to be critiqued and scrutinized. That way, we can know that the data collected is, in fact, showing what we thought it showed.

"Scientists have been following this method for hundreds of years for the simple reason that it works and works well. Every faculty member here at Sci Hi follows this scientific method, and their work is an inspiration to scientists around the world. But the faculty and the students at Sci Hi aren't here for fame or fortune. In fact, most people will never hear of this school or what its graduates achieve. We keep our focus on science rather than celebrity, and the advances that are being made here are changing billions of lives around the world. I'm so proud of all you do and so happy to celebrate all the great work that was done this term. Let's get started!" Dr. Macron moved aside to let the students take center stage.

First up were the seniors that took part in the Black Hole Challenge. The students had been allowed to use Sci Hi's particle accelerator, buried under the perimeter of Goddard Island. The audience was excited to see if anyone had been able to design a probe that could measure the properties of a black hole. The students' solutions were wildly original, but the team that ultimately won had bonded nanomachines to gas molecules that were sucked into the singularity of a black hole. Each tiny machine could only relay data for a fraction of a second, but when billions of them recorded data in succession, the students were able to create a computer simulation of what it would be like to travel into a black hole. The simulation showed a slightly jerky view of a jet-black sphere surrounded by a sparking blue glow. The focus moved toward the sphere slowly at first but built speed rapidly. Something weird happened when the sphere filled the screen. For a second, the view tilted crazily, and colors shifted rapidly. The motion slowed dramatically. The view stabilized and froze, showing a distorted view of a strange planet with several huge colored rings circling the world in multiple orientations. It wasn't Saturn. It was a completely alien planet, some unknowable distance away in time and space that was visible as the probe shot completely through the black hole and emerged in some other universe. The crowd cheered as the image faded to black.

This is totally lethal, Sid thought. *These people are cheering for stuff that no one* ever *cared about at my other school.* Before, his love of science and next-gen gadgets had always made Sidney an outsider, or at the very least "quirky." But here, he fit right in. He felt like he might even do great things at Sci Hi. More importantly, he thought he would be free to try, even if he failed at first. That was how real scientists worked.

Not to be outdone by the seniors, the juniors concluded their paleobiology presentations by introducing a Neanderthal clone. After extracting DNA from a forty-thousand-year-old tooth, the students had found a way to bring an ancient human ancestor back to life. Their modern-day caveman looked a little wary of being onstage but appeared to be completely comfortable with his new friends. He slapped one of the students on the back in excitement and nearly sent the kid flying off the edge of the stage.

The sophomores had spent the term creating a universal language that could be used to communicate with extraterrestrial life. They hadn't discovered any aliens, but they knew their system worked when they were able to communicate with the world's newest Neanderthal, who exclaimed in a video how much he had enjoyed the cafeteria's tuna-salad sandwiches. The auditorium was abuzz with the possibilities.

Finally, Dr. Macron took the stage to introduce the freshman class. "It is a Sci Hi tradition to have the first-year students present their findings last. They are new to the school, and for many, this is the first time they have been encouraged to solve a problem using the scientific method. We have seen the fascinating projects the upper classes have worked on. And this year, the first-year students had an opportunity to engage in a truly remarkable scientific endeavor. I'm especially excited to have them share their results. The other classes have done their own share of amazing work, but none of the other students have actually entered the worlds they were studying, and their findings could impact the entire world."

To begin the presentations, the teachers discussed the location of the hives each group had visited and then introduced the students as each team presented its data. The hives in Europe and North America displayed the most serious cases of CCD. The images and data the students recorded showed the bees suffering from several different diseases in addition to the varroa mites. Tests of the mites and the larval bees revealed that the mites were responsible for spreading the diseases. One student suggested it was similar to the way rats and fleas spread the plague in the Middle Ages.

Soon, it was time for Dr. Sharp's students. "My students were assigned to study honeybees in Japan, where they have shown no signs of colony collapse disorder, whereas their relatives in North America and Europe are being wiped out by it. The students uncovered some very interesting findings, which we will share with you now."

The first group of students from the Japan field trip mounted the stage and launched their presentation. Seated on the right side of the auditorium, Sid leaned over to Penny. "Are you sure you're up for this? I can run the images since Hari is going to do all the talking. You don't even have to come up onstage if you don't want to."

She shook her head. "I'm fine. I just can't get the sight of all those dead bees out of my head."

Hari's voxpod beeped. "It's our turn. Let's go." They mounted the stage as the audience clapped for the group that had just finished.

Once onstage, Penny used her voxpod to launch their presentation. Hari walked the audience through what they had learned about the Japanese bees removing the larvae and pupae infected by the varroa mites. "This may dramatically reduce the spread of the mites in the hive, which may also reduce the spread of some of the diseases that affect European and North American bees. It isn't clear whether this behavior is the result of a genetic mutation or some sort of newly acquired instinct. Further study will be needed to arrive at the cause."

Hari nodded to Sid, who stepped forward.

"We have one more thing to show. While we were inside, the hive was attacked by giant hornets. We put together a little movie about what happened."

Penny started the movie, which was projected on the walls and the ceiling of the auditorium, giving the viewers a sense of what it was it was like to be in the hive. Penny had edited together the video footage they shot during the hornet attack, with dark, dramatic music added in the background.

When the first giant hornet showed up, the audience gasped as they saw the scale of the huge insect. Sid grinned when the sound effects kicked in. An echoing thud sounded as the hornet moved in, and then a loud roar taken from a very old *kaiju* movie that Sid liked rang out. The audience laughed for a moment, then gasped as the bees mobbed the intruding hornet.

Shaky helmet footage of Penny, Sid, and Hari fighting off the hornets with the shock prods was greeted with wild cheers from the students. As the film went on, the audience grew quiet as footage of the carnage filled the screen. Torn cells, emptied of honey. Bee larvae and pupae ripped open, screaming silently. Thousands of dead bees, some still twitching slightly, spread all around the hive.

When the movie ended, the lights came up. The audience clapped and cheered. The Tesla students stood and cheered the loudest.

Dr. Sharp took to the stage again. "That was truly an amazing experience. I would like to commend the students, Sidney Jamison, Hari Gupta, and Penny Day, for staying calm in such a difficult situation. We were all very fortunate. Those giant hornets are responsible for a tragic number of deaths every year in Japan. Luckily, no one was hurt...."

"How can you say that?!" Penny shouted angrily. Her voice echoed in the silent hall. "Forty thousand bees were killed! They didn't stand a chance, even when we were helping them! If we'd had more batteries, maybe we could've held them off...." Her voice broke.

"Oh, my," Dr. Sharp said, unsure what to do.

Dr. Macron quickly strode to the front of the auditorium and mounted the steps. She reached Penny and hugged her tightly. The robot floating over the stage picked up her soothing voice.

"Penny, you've been through a very difficult experience. I know that kind of destruction is hard to witness. You must remember, though, that the bees, and the hornets, too, are behaving just as they evolved to. We consider the bees beneficial because they pollinate flowers and crops that we value. I understand that you view the hornets as bad because they attacked the bees. As a person, I can sympathize with how you feel. As a scientist, though, I must stay objective. The hornets were just using their adaptations to help them to survive. Those adaptations include the way they prey on honeybees. The hornets aren't doing it to be mean or vicious. They're doing it because that's what their instincts have directed them to do, the same way the honeybees' instincts direct them to gather pollen and produce honey. Scientists must take their emotions out of the situation, recording the facts of what occurs. Sometimes, it can be very difficult to do, but we must strive to do so."

Penny nodded, still visibly upset.

"The honeybees weren't totally destroyed," Dr. Sharp broke in. "Before we left, I sent in my assistant Verge to check on the status of the hive. The hornets never made it deep enough into the nest to find the queen. You held off the hornets. They left the hive before their campaign was completed. There were still a few worker bees left. They will rebuild the colony in time."

"Really?" Penny looked up at him hopefully. "I didn't know that." She smiled at Sidney and Hari.

Dr. Sharp continued, "Yes, but it's important to remember science isn't about controlling the world. It's about observing and understanding it. For the information we collect to be meaningful, it must be objective. Our personal beliefs and biases must be kept out of our experiments for accurate results. Sometimes, though, we change the very thing we observe just by observing it. The hornet attack was a natural phenomenon that we should have simply observed, not interfered with...."

"But the circumstances must be considered," Dr. Macron added. "Scientists have the right to defend their own lives. We can't forget that we scientists are people. We're not machines. We're not computers. And unlike bees, we don't always follow the rules. Our process, and we ourselves, may not be perfect. But we try, and strive, and forge ahead. Not every experiment turns out the way we think it will, but that is part of the journey and the discovery of science."

Dr. Macron's words echoed in Sidney's head. He hoped his journey with science was just beginning. There was nothing easy about attending Sci Hi, but he knew it was the first step down a path that led somewhere worth traveling. He remembered his mom's encouraging words. He couldn't wait to tell her about Sci Hi and his new friends. He knew she would be proud of all he had done. Sidney thought ahead to what the next terms at Sci Hi would bring. Aliens? Mutant body parts? Time travel?

Before his mind could float too far away, he was brought back to Earth by Dr. Sharp's voice ringing out in the auditorium. "All right, everyone, I believe we have come to the moment you've all been waiting for—the winners of the coveted Sci Hi Prizes. And since I know you'll all be too excited to listen once we get going, I'll just say now that I have enjoyed this term immensely and look forward to welcoming you all back next semester. I can't wait to see what you discover next.

"And now without further ado!" Dr. Sharp continued. "Each term, awards are presented in the categories of biology, cosmology, physics, and chemistry. For those of you new to Sci Hi, I can tell you that past winners of the Sci Hi Prize have gone on to make amazing contributions to the sciences, and many have received Nobel Prizes for their work. Dr. Vary, if you would announce the awards, please?"

Dr. Vary climbed the stairs to the stage to announce the winners, starting with the seniors first. Each student called to the stage received a round of thunderous applause. Talos was on hand to present a large crystal trophy etched with the Sci Hi emblem to students who had made breakthroughs in fighting deadly outbreaks of the Ebola virus and a team that had found new ways to store data in a strand of DNA.

"And now we have the results of the Great Mutation Challenge," Dr. Vary announced.

Sidney shot his friends a grin and Penny waved her crossed fingers.

"In third place is Team Omnivore with its *vacupotamus*." An image of a huge creature balanced on hundreds of tiny legs appeared on the viewscreen. Its head was flat and wide, perfect for sucking up plants or small animals on the ground. The audience cheered.

"Second place was taken by Team Botanicide with its *snaretree*." An image of a thick tree with dense branches that drooped down to the ground appeared. A small, cute deer-like creature was grazing near the tree. Suddenly, one of the branches jerked upward, yanking the deer off the ground, trapping it in a leafy "net" to be digested. The students applauded.

Dr. Vary spoke again. "Finally, the top prize goes to an organism that has thrived no matter what the environmental conditions or available food source. It was programmed to follow very simple rules that produced powerful results. The winner of the virtual biosphere simulation for this term is…Team Biopocalypse with its *eyeball parasite*!"

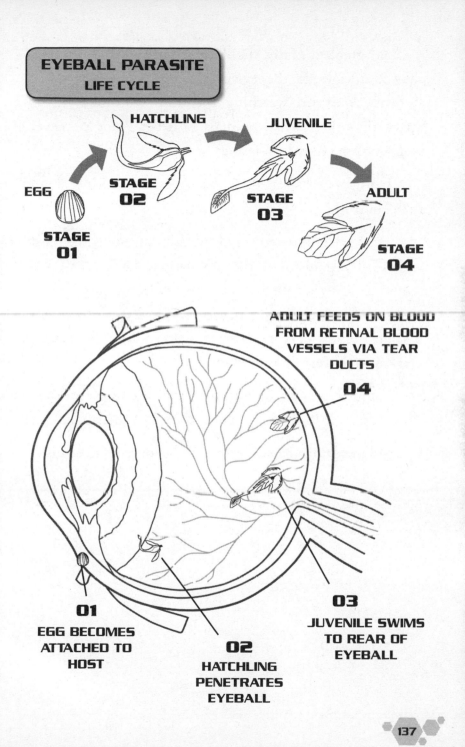

EYEBALL PARASITE
LIFE CYCLE

HATCHLING

JUVENILE

EGG

STAGE
02

STAGE
03

ADULT

STAGE
01

STAGE
04

ADULT FEEDS ON BLOOD
FROM RETINAL BLOOD
VESSELS VIA TEAR
DUCTS

04

01
EGG BECOMES
ATTACHED TO
HOST

02
HATCHLING
PENETRATES
EYEBALL

03
JUVENILE SWIMS
TO REAR OF
EYEBALL

Sid grabbed Hari's shoulder. "That's us!" The screen showed images of the eyeball parasite's life cycle. The students squirmed watching the little wormlike things attack the other virtual animals. "I'll bet Pradeep's never won anything like this, has he?"

Hari looked startled. "I wasn't even thinking about that!" he said.

Dr. Vary continued, "The eyeball parasite is the most successful organism in the simulation, having infected almost eighty percent of all the creatures in the biosphere. It has spread to every landmass in an absurdly short amount of time. Because of that, I award the title of Most Successful Organism to Team Biopocalypse!"

Penny, Hari, and Sid ran back on stage to accept their trophy from Talos as the students cheered and clapped.

Sid raised his fists in victory and shouted, "Eyeballs!"

Reader's Guide

Questions for the Author

A life-long sci-fi fan, Timothy J. Bradley is happy to bring the big, weird, and wild side of science fiction to a new generation. He lives with his wife and son in Southern California, where he can't help but wonder "What if…" every time he looks out the window.

When did you realize you wanted to be a writer?

I didn't actually think about writing books until about ten years ago. I had wanted to illustrate children's books, but I hadn't had any luck getting projects. I finally decided that it might help if I were to write my own book and illustrate it. I was able to find a publisher, and the experience was so fun that I just kept writing!

What's the best advice you've ever received about writing?

Reading is really important for an author. I like to see how other writers structure a story and handle things like plot and dialogue. I often reread paragraphs or descriptions in books I like.

You're both the author and illustrator of Hive Mind. *How does this affect the way you work?*

I'm an artist first, and I tend to think in images and "movie clips" when I think about a story—almost like puzzle pieces. Writing the story is a matter of arranging the puzzle pieces in the right order and typing it into my computer. Once I have a first draft of a book done, I go back and see what is still missing or might need to be described in more detail. I do lots of little sketches as I write, and those usually end up being the start of any illustrations in the book.

What character in Hive Mind *is most like you?*

I'd have to say that I have a bit of Sidney in me. When I was younger, I was always frustrated in school because we weren't learning anything interesting, especially in science! It drove me crazy. I never complained the way Sidney does at the beginning of the book, but I thought about doing it lots of times. That made that particular scene really fun to write.

If you were a student at Sci Hi, what would you study?

Biology, definitely. Or maybe astronomy. But paleontology would be cool. Physics and chemistry are really interesting, too. And anthropology, for sure. Or maybe….

Can we look forward to more Sci Hi books?

Absolutely! I have more adventures in mind for the students at Sci Hi to get involved in. I'm writing the next book right now.

Questions from the Hive

The questions below aren't a quiz or an assignment. There's no right answer to these questions. And that means there's no wrong answers to these questions, either. They're just a way to get your mind buzzing as you think about the world of *Hive Mind*.

- Have you ever taken apart something you were curious about? What happened?

- The title *Hive Mind* refers to the swarm intelligence that social animals like bees, hornets, and fish display. What examples of swarm intelligence are seen in the book?

- How does swarm intelligence differ from the type of individual decisions humans usually make? In what ways does swarm intelligence offer an advantage? In what ways is it limiting?

- Why do you think Sidney dreams his legs are turning into stone on page 79? In what ways does it relate to the changes in his life? In what ways does this passage foreshadow the confrontation with the hornet in Chapter 7?

- At the end of the book, how did Dr. Macron and Dr. Sharp address the three friends' concerns about the bees? What would you have told Penny? Think about the different opinions held by the friends about the bees' deaths. Which most closely agrees with your own view?

In what ways is *Hive Mind* similar to other books you've read? Which books does it remind you of? In what ways are the sci-fi details in *Hive Mind* similar to or different from these books?

If you were a student at Sci Hi, what kind of activity, experiment, or field trip would you like to take part in?

The Science of Sci Hi

Some of the science-fiction elements in *Hive Mind*, such as voxpods and the intermaze, were inspired by today's tablet computers and Internet. Others, like the postal-delivery bot, may one day be real but aren't yet a part of our world. Read on to sort fact from fiction.

CCD Causes

Colony collapse disorder is a real and serious danger, and scientists are studying what causes CCD and how to prevent it. Pesticides, viruses, and human actions are all being investigated as possible causes. Varroa mites spread a deadly form of deformed wing virus and are considered a leading cause of CCD.

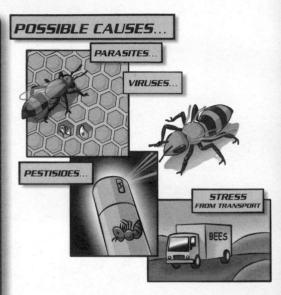

POSSIBLE CAUSES...

PARASITES...

VIRUSES...

PESTISIDES...

STRESS FROM TRANSPORT

BEES

Bee Balls

Hornets are a constant threat to bees. Bee stingers are too small to penetrate the hornets' exoskeletons. To fight back against the giant Asian hornet, bees have been seen forming a what is called a "hot defensive bee ball." When hundreds of bees vibrate together, the bee ball cooks the hornet to death over the course of an hour.

Meaningful Messages

Bees use movement and pheromones to communicate with one another. They are famous for the "dance" they use to direct one another to the best flowers. Each movement is interpreted by the other bees, and if they disagree, they may head-butt each other. Pheromones are special chemicals the bees emit. Each one produces a specific scent that spreads a message such as "Come over here" or "I'm the queen."

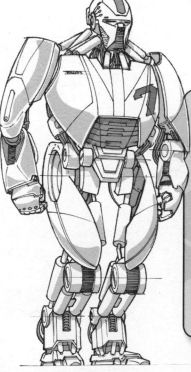

True Tech

Computer programmers are already developing artificial forms of intelligence that can make decisions and judgments the same way the human brain does. And nanobots are being developed for use by doctors to scan and repair the human body.

Make It Your Own

If you loved reading *Hive Mind*, let the world know! Get creative. Try the activities below, or come up with your own way to show off your Sci Hi pride.

Collect and Reflect

Create Pinterest boards for each character. Pin art, videos, science reports, and gadgets that would fascinate and inspire Sidney, Penny, and Hari.

The Perfect Fit

Paint a dark T-shirt with a quote from your favorite character. Grab a bleach pen (and an adult) and start drawing.

Lights, Camera, Action!

Make a book trailer that highlights the most exciting moments in the book. Use the camera on your phone, or create a montage in a video app online.

Another Take

Create a comic-book version of a scene from the book. Work out what moments are most important and deserve close-ups. Create speech bubbles and thought bubbles to show how the characters are feeling.

Pop Quiz

Take this quick quiz to find out which Sci Hi character you resemble the most.

In a hundred years, you would love to see

A) a robot president

B) a cure for cancer

C) an international school for geniuses

On weekends, you're most likely to be found

A) working on a bike in the garage

B) playing soccer

C) at the library

When you grow up, you want to be

A) an inventor

B) a sports doctor

C) an astronaut

Answers:
Mostly As: You are curious and ready for adventure. You're most like Sidney. **Mostly Bs:** You are athletic, impatient, and caring. You're most like Penny. **Mostly Cs:** You are thoughtful and friendly. You're most like Hari.

Schedule Scramble

Read the assignments and guess which Sci Hi class you're in. The answers are below.

1) Investigate the different ways bacteria and viruses affect the human body—from inside the human body. Don't be afraid to ask big questions!

2) Travel back in time to observe how our ancestors lived 40,000 years ago. Submit your report by Friday. Disturbances in the space-time continuum will result in the loss of 10 points from the final grade.

3) Breed animals to learn more about their strongest traits. Try crossing a walrus with a peacock or a shark with a gorilla. Data will be recorded using Sci Hi's exclusive THING 2.0 software.

4) Combine engineering skills with physical strength to create a mile-long tunnel underground. The first person to complete the task receives the *A*. Teamwork is encouraged.

5) Design a message to be sent to another universe. Communication devices must be able to withstand intense forces and unpredictable changes in the number of dimensions supported by the universe. Prototypes due Tuesday.

Answers:
1) Microbiology 2) Paleobiology 3) Mutations 4) Physical Education 5) Black Hole Studies